LILT LITERARY
BECAUSE BOOKS BELONG
TO THEIR READERS

L.C. SPOERING

At the Edge of the World

L.C. Spoering

LILT LITERARY

BECAUSE BOOKS BELONG
TO THEIR READERS

This is a work of fiction. Names, characters, places, and incidents either are the product of the author's imagination or are used fictitiously, and any resemblance to any persons, living or dead, business establishments, events, or locales is entirely coincidental.

AT THE EDGE OF THE WORLD

ISBN-10: 0996005455
ISBN-13: 978-0-9960054-5-6

First E-Book Edition: August, 2014
First Print Edition: September, 2014

www.liltliterary.com

AT THE EDGE OF THE WORLD

For the freaks, for the kids who never fit in, for everyone destined for better things.

CHAPTER ONE

Shane had not been hard, or jaded, or even all that angry the day he landed on the beach. His story was not unique. They were a dime a dozen out there, unremarkable enough that he was ignored by most of the street rats who moved in packs up and down the beach, their own form of infestation.

There was a shame in that, and Shane was prone to weaving extra layers to his story, staying away from an outright lie but taking poetic license, as it were, to thread a sense of discontent, alienation, agony where there was none. It was the false gold thread on his shit tapestry whip-stitched to detract from the fact that there was very little to it to begin with.

Shane had been Levron when he first arrived in Venice at the age of fifteen. He was worn down on the heels of his sneakers in what had gone from turn of phrase into the physical reality of running away. He was dressed in the same clothes he'd skipped town in: a hooded sweatshirt, jeans and those shoes, which were now faded at the insignias, the rubber soles flaking apart under the weight of his winnowing body.

He had only been in Venice for three days before he was picked up, having no sense about him as how to dodge the police in a place that was so wide-open. He was intoxicated with the scene, with that expanse of sand that

1

seemed to crawl up to the brightly-colored buildings and people that lined the walk. He was practically blind in that light, in the reflected sun off the waves and bared skin, like a child who'd been raised in a bomb shelter, stumbling onto the line between the wild and civilization, confused as to which was which. He'd followed the packs of street kids at a distance, and spent the evenings out of their circle. He'd curled against the shocking wind off the water in his hoodie, hands deep in the kangaroo pockets, fingering the apartment key he carried, still, on its lanyard. It was obvious he didn't belong, not just there, but anywhere, and it came as little surprise to him when he was jumped near the pier.

Levron had never been in a fight. It wasn't just something his mother discouraged, but outright forbid, and the one time another boy came running that Levron had pushed him, when they were all of eight years old, she'd snatched him by the ear and tossed him in his room without supper. The next morning had found him relieved of all his toys for the next two weeks. Violence, his mother had informed him, was something that dismantled the soul, made you less of a person with each hit landed. She wanted to build him up, not watch him break down.

Instinct had him curl into a ball the instant he hit the sand; the first punch had landed like a rock thrown to his belly, sending shocking waves of pain throughout his core. It was unlike any pain he'd ever experienced, until the next blow hit him, at his chin, and his brain simply rebelled.

He was landed upon, swarmed. He would never be sure exactly how many there were, as fists seemed to come out of nowhere, produced out of thin air. Sneakers with rubber toes seemed to turn into deadly spikes, driving into the softness of his sides, the resistance of his ribs.

"We're the welcoming committee!" one trilled as a fist dove into that first abused spot, somehow increasing and dulling the pain at once. The amassed kids all groaned, as if this was a joke they'd heard one too many times, but Shane almost chuckled at the absurdity of it all, at the fact he'd come this far, thousands of miles, just to die on the beach he'd been seeking for so long.

He was aware of this, of impending death, in a way he hadn't been in his entire life. He could taste it in the blood at the back of his throat, hear it in the ringing of his ears, feel it in the gob of spit lobbed onto his cheek. It oozed over his broken skin like a slug, and while Levron awaited that killing blow, the blackness dropped down over his eyes like a mask.

The next time he opened his eyes, he was alone with the pain. He rolled onto his back and managed to make out the crescent moon hanging in the sky like scythe, the stars obscured by the lights of the city so that it was the only thing above him. He laid there, breaths sending a crackling pain through his ribs, until a cop leaned over him and blocked his view.

He was sat up, a blanket draped around his shoulders. Later, he would realize that he didn't look the part at the time, the part of a street kid, still too green and tidy. That was why he was afforded the kindness of warmth and an emergency ice pack for his swollen eye, a paramedic to dab at the cut on his forehead and his crushed nose. He was lead up the beach and tended to with a tenderness he could only connect to that of a mother's love, and he cried over his wounds, into the rawness of scraped palms, a sudden wave of loneliness and need so overwhelming, he could barely breathe.

One of the cops asked for his address, so they could get him home. It was a generosity that would not be extended in subsequent busts down the road, but, at the time, he did not know that. He knew nothing about the area, of LA or Santa Monica, and barely anything about Venice itself, half-surprising himself when he arrived there, even, as though he'd appeared, like magic.

As lies went, the one he presented to the cops that

night wasn't much of one at all: he couldn't go home because his step-dad hit him. Leaving out the distance qualified it as one in his mind, one of the first he had any real memory of telling. When the officer in front of him exchanged a look with the one behind him, Levron felt his stomach twist hard enough to make him gag. He stuffed a hand, covered with a gauze pad and tape, against his mouth and willed himself not to puke.

"What's your name, son?" It was a question he would eventually anticipate but, in his opinion, no kid had ever started out hardened. His shoulders rounded, and his throat ached, and he was shivering in the wind that came up off the ocean.

"Shane." It was a name pulled out of thin air, maybe a name from a kid in a class, but once it was out of his mouth, it became affixed to his being, if just to make it one less lie to burden himself with.

"Shane, how old are you?"

He picked at the edge of the tape, considered. "Almost eighteen." Each new lie landed with a thud on his shoulders. "Next week."

Another glance was exchanged, and he tried to read the unspoken between the two men, clearly already wearied by the evening. A lump of a man trundled by, pushing his shopping cart of possessions, urged on by another uniformed officer.

"It's not curfew yet," the squatting one finally said; they didn't believe him, but there was something in his tone that made Shane's heart leap and thud against the back of his throat.

"You can't stay down here on the beach." The officer straightened up, stretched his back. At that angle, Shane could see his gun, glinting under the sulfur light of the street lamp above their heads, and it illuminated the area in a sickly orange shade.

"You should really sleep off that beating," he added,

giving the teenager a stern look.

It struck Shane he was probably a father and, as things went, likely not a bad guy. Shane was soft, his mother's son, and he'd never quite had the capacity to distrust someone on sight.

That night, he gave the cops a shaken smile. "I'll find my way home," he promised, keeping his voice as flat as possible, a poor attempt to sound like the surfers he'd heard during the day, the greased-up weight lifters, something as watery as the sea.

"You do that, son." The officer nodded at the gel pack Shane was still holding to his injured eye, somewhat like a security blanket. "Why don't you keep that till you get home, huh?"

Another tremulous smile. "Thanks."

He pushed himself to his feet; he felt oddly uninjured at every other point, blood buzzing through his veins, head light. Maybe it wouldn't be so bad after all.

He had the power to maneuver out of the cops' range of view, closer to the lights of the city. They were busy enough, he supposed, as the men turned to talk to each other when he glanced back.

He stopped under the artificial darkness of an overhanging palm tree and moved the gel pack from his eye; it was thick and warm, despite the icing, and swollen shut under his fingertips. With his good eye, though, he still saw her.

She was peering from around the edge of a large, graffiti-strewn sculpture, the streetlights unable to reach her. He would have missed her too, but for the shift of her hair under the moon, turning it into twists of silver, her eyes, too, and they met his one good one for a long beat before she turned and vanished entirely, a ghost in the night.

CHAPTER TWO

She was a sight on Venice Beach just like all the others, another presence that made up the tapestry of weirdos who occupied the strange strip along the coast.

Tall, skinny, wearing skin-tight jeans and tank-top, she wore skates on her feet like born appendages, rolling as natural as walking was for others. No one had ever seen her without them, and, truly, no one had ever really seen her still, but for Shane.

There were regulars down on the beach, he learned over the years, like landmarks for tourists: fire-breathers and a one-man-band, a painter sitting on the ground, warring ventriloquists. There were the bodybuilders, a zoo unto themselves, and gutterpunks on skateboards performing death-defying tricks. There were girls with their swimsuits painted on, a guy who wore a seven foot boa constrictor like a scarf.

And, always, around the edges, the streetfolk, as easily ignored as the native plant life that had taken a backseat to the spectacle of the rest of the boardwalk.

Shane was almost seventeen when he realized that reality: a tourist pitched a cup in his direction, the thing bouncing off his brow harmlessly. It wasn't a malicious gesture: he'd been mistaken for a garbage can.

He'd spent two years living there; Shane had stretched taller, grown into those wide shoulders and large hands —

it had been a good long time since he'd been jumped. He kept tidy, maybe in some form of defiance, washing his spare clothes when he had the change, going shirtless when the weather got hot to spare his tops the sweat.

Just like the other street rats, he'd learned how the beach worked, how the cops moved, and, for the most part, how to keep a few steps ahead. The sheer number of freaks that occupied Venice Beach at any given time made this easier than it probably was in other places, but Shane didn't know other places: he never quite allowed the ocean out of his sight.

Sometimes Shane slept on the beach — the cops knew him by then, the boy who stood a head and shoulders over most of the rats who ran in packs up and down the boardwalk, picking pockets and hocking large gobs of spit in front of tourists. Shane was the one without a pack and, likely, that was why they gave him an allowance they didn't give the other kids. When he was caught, which was often, they just sent him on his way. He always had a place to stay, even when the night was late or the weather rough: Shane, like the girl on the skates, the firebreather, the guy with the snake, was a fixture of the beach, and when he didn't spoil the mood, a freak could stay.

It took him a long time to realize this, that he was included in the numbers that stood out and blended in. He was a trashcan, an invisible, to those from out of town, but some kind of necessary element to the regulars. This made no sense: he did not have a guitar to play, or a pet to look after. He was tall, and had wide shoulders and big hands, skin nearing the color of asphalt from long days in the sun. He was every cliché of a threat, but for the sweet, easy smile that tended to spread, unbidden, over cheeks that stayed packed with baby fat even after many lean years, like a chipmunk perpetually storing for winter.

He was clean for one thing, and he knew that was a bonus. He tied his boots with laces, and rolled up the sleeves of his jacket when they frayed. He strayed away from puddles and washed his hands in the beach showers, his face, and carried a toothbrush in his backpack so that his teeth, though crooked as they'd always been, had a kind of gleam that made the old homeless dude in his wheelchair cackle and shade his eyes every time Shane came into view.

Shane was also polite. He didn't have a skateboard, or an act, didn't speak much. Dollars pressed into his hand were mostly unsolicited, but received with that smile and a sort of murmured thank you. He didn't quite meet the eyes of others, and most took this for respect, and Shane was happy to let them.

He slept at a record shop sometimes, in exchange for mopping their floors after closing, and cleaning the mousetraps in the storage room. The owner was an old stoner named Louis, who bought burgers and rattled off stories about meeting the Beatles when they were hanging with the Maharishi. He tried, on numerous occasions, to teach Shane Transcendental Meditation, which, to him, looked a whole lot like napping.

When it rained, he went to the record shop, and Louis, or his lone employee, Trey, gave him some kind of stocking task, and he was always paid in a handful of small bills and loose change, mostly from the clutch of money Louis kept in a pickle jar in his back office, next to his hookah. The bills always stunk of dill. Once Shane sniffed them to the point of headache, and then he never ate another pickle again.

The guy next door, the owner of the t-shirt shop, didn't like Shane. He was a paunchy man in his late thirties, maybe forties, with a severely receding hairline for which he attempted to compensate by growing his hair down to his shoulders and tying it back in a ponytail. He wore one of his own shirts, day in, day out: a gaudy, bright tie-dyed number with *Venice Beach: Experience It!* emblazoned in Comic Sans across the front. He smoked nasty little cigars and knew a shocking number of racial slurs, many of which Shane had been unaware stood for anything until they came out of the man's mouth.

Louis liked Shane though, or at least, tolerated him. It was a strange sort of fondness, like one might have for a nasty tomcat that shows up at the back door with a new injury every week. He sold him pot and they traded stories about the old days on the boardwalk, and Shane stayed at the back of the store, listening to mixtapes Trey put on and keeping one eye on the street.

He watched for the cops sometimes — they were charged with insuring there were no illegal workers in the shops, though they rarely did much about it — but he mostly watched for the girl on skates.

No one knew her name or where she lived; her clothes rarely changed, but she didn't have the same aura of sweat and sand that the homeless kids all seemed to have. Her jeans tucked into her skates, and her top tucked into her jeans, and, over each hand, she wore fingerless gloves, like a bicyclist, covering her palms and fingers up to her first knuckle. Her hair hung in twists down over her shoulders. It seemed to be silver, but also blue and pink and orange and gold, shifting and shimmering in and out of shadows and sunlight, the flash of the ferris wheel lights, the moon. Her exposed shoulders and neck, cheeks and chin and forehead, shone silver: she was pale white and she wasn't, and some speculated she applied some make-up every day, another costume paraded down the beach.

Shane watched her like he watched the ocean, and the girl on the skates always came rolling down the boardwalk at ten and at four. Sometimes she appeared late in the evening, or early in the morning, but Shane didn't know how often that actually occurred. He'd only seen her once by the dawn, and twice at night, the first time he'd been jumped.

He played that night over in his mind often, trudging

down the sidewalk and turning to see her silver face reflecting the faint light of the moon behind the great pillar decorated with the paint of many artists. She'd held the edge of the sculpture, fingers curled around the cement, and she'd been watching him, he was sure, positive, beyond, though she never seemed to acknowledge him ever again.

Ten and four, he watched the boardwalk and rarely missed her. She slithered between pedestrians with the ease of a snake, the wheels of her skates ringing against the pavement with each push she gave, her shoulders hunched and elbows tight against her sides. She moved swiftly, but without the stance of a racer, as if she were simply built to move fast, and the wheels had attached themselves to her feet to aid her in this.

She skated with the same ease through the rain, even as puddles seemed neck deep and the tall trees were weighted with water. He wondered, from the safety of the record shop, or in the doorway of the shuttered newsstand, if she was ever alarmed by the storms that moved in from the sea, with the lightning that lit the boardwalk like it was a curious sort of day. They scared Shane, and most of the kids who called Venice Beach home. Not the girl on skates: ten and four, she was out there, more dependable than the postal service.

She never looked around; there seemed a singular purpose to her movements, down the sidewalk, whizzing through crowds, vanishing past the end of the main drag. Did she disappear into the canals, the neighborhood of aging houses behind the strip? He never followed to ask.

CHAPTER THREE

Venice, California, had started out as a resort town, back when people had the time and money for that sort of thing. To the people who now occupied the strip of land a hundred years later, the founding of the place was no more than a distant memory. Indeed, most of the actual residents, the street rats and circus freaks and blue collar workers, didn't even know why it was named for a storied city in Italy.

The beach was a separate entity from the actual city, in the eyes of those who dwelled there, on either side of the divide. One of the wealthiest neighborhoods in Los Angeles, it was only the pier that saw any mingling of the groups, and, to Shane, it appeared everyone was just fine with the arrangement.

In truth, the neighborhood made him uncomfortable, and only a part of that was the distance from the ocean. It was an attitude he'd found in kind with the other kids who shuttled from the sand to the sidewalk and back again over the course of the days, even as he was hardly as entrenched in the culture as they seemed to be.

There was a hierarchy on the street, in a way that made little sense to him, except to know that he was either on the bottom, or considered a whole other creature, unlike them. Shane was older, and Shane had not been out on his own as long. Two years was nothing to some of them, even the skinny thirteen year olds just starting to sprout wiry hairs from their acne-ridden chins. Two years was just getting started, and some of the other kids had been running away from homes and foster homes and group homes since they could walk. Some of them had been a beach kid for five, six years by the time their voices changed.

Shane had a system that made him invisible at night, one that made his back hurt like an old man's when he got up in the morning from the low casement window around the corner from one of the store fronts. As tall as he was, Shane was thin, and curling into small spaces had become something of a second nature within weeks of arriving in California. The window well was a place that was easy to miss, and, thus, easy for Shane to claim, and keep warm and dry and somewhat clean by the careful arrangement of a blanket he kept in the bottom of his backpack.

Mornings found him emerging like a prairie dog, head and shoulders first, and then the rest of him as he pulled himself up and out the last feet up onto the asphalt. He could smell the ocean from there, over the rot from the dumpsters, and, when he craned his neck, he could see it, too, a strangely important fact. He didn't understand his own compulsion, except that the ocean was where he faced most of the day, and what he needed like the beat of his heart.

By habit, he was up at dawn, before the trash truck rumbled into the alley, and before the cops came through the neighborhood, street by street, rustling the homeless people up. Shane gathered up his stuff, and made his spot sufficiently unimpressive before moving back onto the promenade. That was where a tiny woman always appeared, pushing along a small trolley from which she sold baked goods: Mexican pastries, flakey and coated in sugar. Shane would use his change to buy egg bread coated in strawberry frosting, bright pink, dissolving on his tongue like magic, inexplicably still warm despite the lady having traveled miles to sell on the boardwalk.

Coffee came from pairs of bright-eyed, fresh-faced kids not much older than he was: missionaries, he'd figured out eventually, despite their inability to really express the word of the Gospel when confronted with a gang of thirteen year old huffers. Shane would have listened, but he seemed to scare them the most, and they handed him a Styrofoam cup, steaming hot, before backing away in a hurry. He never stopped them, though, at first, months and months before, there was a permeating sense of guilt about it. Guilt wasn't all that useful out there; it was yet another thing he'd outgrown.

Mornings were easy on the beach, warm and hazy like the sunrise, and he found himself near the water's edge before too long, despite never venturing in.

The trouble, of course, was that Shane couldn't swim. At some point, his mother had tried to teach him, had taken him out on the rickety dock of the river-fed lake near some campground they'd stayed at for weeks when he was young. She stood in the water that came up to her shoulders and urged him in, but he was struck by a fear that clenched in his chest, deep and dark and intense, and, finally, she gave up. He could stand on the bank, and cast rocks and sticks into the water, but he would not go in.

Until the night he did. It wasn't too late, not really, and his mother was off having a cigarette. His feet led him naturally down to the banks, like someone had taken his hand, and where he counted the stars reflected on the surface before throwing a rock in, and counted them again when the ripples shattered them into pieces. Maybe it was that dashing of the lights, or the still of the evening, cool that close to the water. The only real sound was crickets somewhere in the reeds, but he was up to his knees before he noticed. With a recklessness seen only in boys that small, he dove in all at once, feet in the air, and then he was gone.

He couldn't swim. What he could do was sink, and he did that in short order, without thrashing or fear. He just sank, the weight of his clothes dragging him to the bottom, along with the rocks and roots and discarded car parts, under the black of the water. When his mother found him, frantic, he was laid on the sand of the beach, barely conscious, sputtering, but fine. He had no idea how he got there, if some burst of adrenaline overrode the fact that he did not have the skill to kick and stroke, or if there was some divine intervention, but he survived, and his mother made him swear never to go near the water again.

He could not obey that command, but he never went in again, never even took off his shoes to allow the tide to lap at his toes. His sneakers stayed firmly on his feet even then, watching the Pacific turn from black to indigo to blue, and when he saw the girl trudging up the beach, away from the pier, he didn't move either.

It only struck him, the closer she got to him, that he'd never seen her without her skates. Indeed, looking down at her feet, he could discern they were bare, sinking into the sand with each step; her hands were covered with fingerless gloves of a lacy variety, nearly up to her elbows. Her shirt was tight and shimmering like the scales of a fish in the early morning light, and her legs were covered in a shiny fabric, snug as paint on a wall. Her hair trailed down over her shoulders and chests; he'd never noticed the length, as fast as she moved, but it was to her elbows, and looked both like water and to be in great, gnarled tangles at once.

He could see her face the closer she got, and the way her expression changed as he glanced at her, in sips, trying to appear like he wasn't staring at her approach. Her face had been slack, vacant, but, as she grew in perspective, he saw that she looked worried, a little dismayed, eyes widening so that they shone like a cat in oncoming high beams.

Still, she closed the distance between them, and stopped several feet away, feet sunk deep in the sand, her arms limp at her side, the strands of hair around her face dancing in the bracing breeze that lifted off the moderate waves before them.

"I come out here every morning," he finally ventured, trying to ignore how it felt as though his heart was doing a tap dance in his throat. "To watch the sun rise."

She didn't respond, and the silence went on for so long that he wondered if she'd slipped away silently. Shane looked up, and found himself startled by her proximity, just a few inches away, looking down at him with such an intensity, it felt almost violating.   "Yeah?" It was the first word he'd ever heard her speak, and it was disappointing: short and soft, so that he could not hear her tone, accent, nothing—it was as mutable and unidentifiable as water.

He shrugged, a buzzing running along his nerves. "Can't sleep that late." For plenty of reasons.

"Yeah." A near-identical echo as the one before, and he looked down at the sand that was creeping in through the lace grommets of his sneakers, disappointed, though he didn't know why.

He heard her shift, and then, to his utter shock, she sat down on the sand next to him, drawing her knees up to her chest. She was longer than he had realized, long and thin, cool and smooth.

"I…" He had nothing to say and, after another beat, held up the mostly intact pastry he'd only picked at. "Wanna share?"

Her head turned to rest her cheek against a bony knee, and he saw, finally, up close, her eyes were grey. "Share?" Her lips were grey, too, or silver, a pink so pale in the dawn light they were rendered almost colorless.

He offered it again, holding it closer, higher, this time. "It's real good. A lady up on the boardwalk makes 'em every morning. It's still warm."

She didn't move, though he could feel her breath, see

17

the slight rise and fall of her shoulders. She seemed exhausted, weary in a way that should have been etched on her face, but seemed to only come out through the way she held herself, her hoarse, hesitant voice.

Finally, she unwound one long arm from around her bent legs and reached out to break a small piece of the sweet bread away from the rest. Her fingertips were almost blue, the cold, he thought, and her fingernails bitten to the quick.

Shane's eyes followed the pastry to her mouth, those pale lips. He watched it touch the cracked skin there, but no bite was taken. She seemed to inhale the aroma instead, before handing it back to him.

"Thanks." She laid her cheek against her knees again, and he looked down at the roll, as though it were suddenly sainted, and he couldn't eat another bite.

"I... You're not usually down here," he said, finally. That he'd never seen her outside her ten and four route along the pavement made the meeting all the more confusing. He spent every morning drinking coffee and eating the pastry, sometimes with a pilfered cigarette, always alone.

She breathed out, and he thought it might have been intended as a laugh.

"Really? I feel like I'm here all the time." With those words, a fuller picture formed, and it didn't: she had no accent to speak of, and the voice she used was rough and smooth at once. Her voice sounded like what the pink frosting tasted like, the texture of sugar granules melting on his tongue.

He set the roll down carefully on the paper napkin he'd kept pinned under the toe of his sneaker, and then wiped his fingertips on his jeans. "I've only ever seen you skate by."

Finally, she smiled, an upturn of that nearly-invisible mouth, and it was sweet and small and smooth, like her skin, pushing dimples high up on her cheeks. "Everybody does," she said, and then her smile sank and her eyes, grey as the ocean, looked over the water.

"You're really good." It was a lame compliment, and Shane knew it, and he wanted to stuff it back down, especially when she sighed out, stretched her legs, sending her hair tumbling down her back to brush the ends over the sand.

"I should go." In one movement, a ripple from toe to the top of her head, she rose, curling her arms around herself, hands cupping elbows, like she might break apart onto the sand if she didn't hold on tightly.

"Okay," he said, mouth forming the oh and only barely pushing out the last sound.

She lifted a small foot and touched the rubber edge of his shoe; her toes were pebble-like, purple and grey nails. "Thanks." Before he could answer, she had stepped over him, sand scattering over the roll, and continued on her path as though she'd not stopped next to him at all.

CHAPTER FOUR

That afternoon brought a storm that sent the rain down in sheets so heavy and thick, that even if the girl in skates was out there, Shane wasn't sure he'd be able to see her anyway.

He stood in the window of the record shop, face all but pressed to the glass. Four o'clock, and never once had Shane seen her skip her route along the promenade, not seen her spin by, that hair with colors that defied description and legs flashing like quicksilver on the wheels that carried her down the boardwalk at lightning speed. Rain or shine, even threat of tsunami, she was there, and had been for the entire two years Shane had been squatting in Venice. Something settled, heavy and painful, around his chest at her absence from the afternoon scene.

The minutes ticked by, and he moved away from the window. The store was abandoned but for the three of them, Shane and Louis and Trey. The shuttered doors made the ever-present dust thicker in the air, its own living being, stifling and cool to the touch. He dragged his finger through a thick layer of it over an old, unused hi-fi, the imitation wood oddly glowing where the dirt was wiped away.

Blowing the dust from the tip of his finger, Shane ambled back to the center of the store. Trey was somewhere up in the rafters, like a shop rat, in stores of items only he knew the history of, and Louis perched on his high stool behind the counter, rolling, on the stained leg of his jeans, a sloppy cigarette.

He smoked aromatic tobacco, apple, usually, and his hands were gnarled with something disturbing that came with age. They shook when he rolled his cigarettes, the delicate paper wrinkling and, sometimes, buckling under his fingertips. Shane thought to offer help only once, but Louis, despite his body's visible deterioration, had a sharp gaze, cutting and true, and Shane, really, was afraid of what the old man might see in him.

That afternoon, even before the rain came on, Shane had been going through a bucket of stereo fixtures, and settled back on his lower stool near Louis to do so. The old man finished his task and lit up, nudging Shane with his toe.

"You been quiet." He breathed in deep of his tobacco, lips pursing around the tube, lumpen as it was.

Shane flashed him an insincere smile. "Just one of those days." Truthfully, he wasn't a talker, never had been, and his mind was replaying that morning on the beach over and over, a movie on a loop, and that made it difficult to talk. He analyzed his words, and how he could have said them differently and, by that hour of the day, he was reimagining the conversation with an alternate set of responses — but she still barely spoke.

It was a maddening lack of imagination, maybe, or maybe she was too complex for him to arrange a script for.

Louis snorted. "It's that girl, huh?"

Shane, who had returned his attention to the bucket, looked up sharply. "What girl?" He couldn't keep the suspicion from his voice: it was inborn, and cultivated, and, in those times, those situations, it was clear which one of them lived on the streets and which one had a bed and pillow, and rent to pay.

Louis, though, was undeterred; the street kids had

never scared him, least of all Shane, who always appeared to him like a pitbull — trainable to be vicious and empty, but just as likely as any other dog to roll over to expose a belly and beg for a treat.

"What girl? The one on skates. What other girl would I be talking about?" He sucked in another drag, the burning moving up the paper with a crackling sound like wet wood in a fire.

"There are lots of girls." Shane's tone was sullen, and his gaze dropped to the knob in his hand, though he had stopped sorting as soon as Louis spoke.

"Well, yeah. But you rush to that window anytime she comes by. Don't blame you," he went on, thoughtfully. "She's something else."

That made Shane shake his head. "I don't do that." He felt more shame at being caught, especially unaware, than anything else.

"Get up here," Louis commanded, waving his hand and staring at Shane until the boy set aside the bucket and got to his feet, leaning his rear against the flat side of the glass-fronted case, folding his arms over his chest. Louis, seated, did not come near to Shane's even reposed height.

Louis busied himself, then, reaching into the cooler he always kept at his feet, withdrawing two water-beaded cans of beer and a couple half sandwiches wrapped in plastic. The cigarette wavered in the corner of his mouth.

Immediately, Shane raised his hands in refusal and the old man made a noise at the back of his throat, thick and annoyed. "You been working all morning. Just fucking eat."

What could Shane say to that? He'd only had those couple bites of the pastry that morning and his stomach rolled when he saw the sandwiches, begging like a dog. He reached for the one he thought smaller and carefully unwrapped it: ham and cheese, bright yellow mustard, bread white and soft.

"You ever pray?" he found himself asking Louis as he

23

bit into the sandwich.

Louis cracked open one of the cans. "All the time. Pray to the toilet in the mornings, and the coffee pot once I make it to the kitchen." His smile was wicked, and the gaps between his teeth seemed to have grown since Shane had first met him, like canyons in his mouth.

"Pray to the sun that it stays clear for business," he added, nodding at the door with a brief scowl before his attention was caught by the beer and he took an appreciative sip.

That was a good enough answer, Shane supposed.

"So, do you?"

He swallowed; the sandwich was nothing remarkable, but anything with meat and cheese was always a little bit like heaven.

"I don't know," he admitted, shrugging, fingering, with his free hand, the cold beer he'd been offered; he didn't know if Louis was aware of how old he was, or if it mattered at all.

"I guess I did when I was a kid. Went to church and all." Even as indifferent as he tried to sound, there was an obvious picking and choosing in his speech, and he kept his eyes on the tab of the can.

"You look like a church boy." Louis knew the street kids, and Shane was not the first one to do menial tasks around the store; not a one chattered easily, not if they planned on surviving longer than a night out there.

His gaze lifted and, instead of an annoyed, shuttered look, Shane smiled. It was the smile of a younger boy, much younger, and many miles away. "Sure I do."

Louis didn't snort, even though Shane had expected him to. He knew the older man believed in things like rock and roll and beautiful women, in the letters that came, infrequently, in the mail.

"You talked to her?"

Maybe it should have taken Shane a moment to

understand who Louis was asking about but, of course, it didn't.

He shrugged. "Just a little. This morning."

"And?" Louis was chewing noisily, breathing heavily through his nose; he smoked too much, and Shane could hear his lungs crackling all through the day with the effort of moving air through them.

"I dunno. She's quiet." That seemed like an insufficient explanation, insufficient description of her voice on the beach that morning, soft like sand, gritty under his fingernails.

"What did you talk about?"

"Nothing, really. Just about the beach." How stupid had he been not to try harder to draw her out, to ask her why she was always on the skates, why she was always on the boardwalk, why she disappeared and reappeared without any appearance in between her designated times? He had been struck dumb when faced with her, but was full of questions when she was only visible behind his closed eyelids.

Louis was silent for a long moment, chewing at his sandwich. "That's something," he said, with no real inflection.

Shane deflated slightly; had he been hoping that Louis would have something of depth and wisdom to impart upon him? That was unlikely, but there it was: Louis, oddly enough, was his only actual friend in Venice.

Shane crumpled the plastic from his sandwich in his palm, then swept up crumbs with the other. He cleaned somewhat compulsively, there at the store, and he carried the trash to the bin around the side of the counter. That was when he saw her.

Out in the sheets of rain, she was a blurry form like she was being slowly washed away by the storm. He froze, and when he had to blink next, she was gone.

CHAPTER FIVE

Shane was not the only person in Venice obsessed, as it were, with the girl on skates.

Trey had lived in a studio apartment with three other guys ever since he arrived in LA at eighteen with a runny nose and twelve dollars in his pocket. He was not a runaway, or much of anything at all, drifting to the West coast like so much flotsam from somewhere in the middle of the US.

The beach attracted him for the same reasons it did everyone else. His first day, Trey, wearing a heavy black coat and jeans and thick boots, sat, slightly ill, on the sand for hours a day. He moved gamely when the cops herded him along, settling again in just a slightly different spot until the next sweep.

Louis picked him up the same way he did Shane later, and Donovan years before, and planted him in the storage room of the record shop to do inventory. After some months, Trey reported regularly, learned to work the ancient register, and there he stayed.

The apartment he shared was, predictably, cramped and filthy and smelled heavily of too many young men who didn't wash nearly enough. For three years now, Trey had been sleeping on a fold-out chair under the front window, where the streetlight cast a yellow glow over his face when he rolled over to look out on their unremarkable street.

They'd gotten the lease by the skin of their teeth and regular applications of weed for the super, dealt by Dash, who wore his hair spiked and eyeliner like armor around his watery blue eyes. Trey had the job, the only job between the four of them: this awarded him the chair, though it was Kevin who got the couch because of his disabilities - though, over the past year and a half, Trey could only discern that meant the other guy's farts made the bathroom impossible to enter for hours after Kevin was finished with it.

Dash and Matt slept on the floor, when they returned sometime in the blue hours of the morning. Trey picked his way over the mine field of their skinny limbs and discarded clothes to leave the apartment in the morning to go to work.

Trey worked in inventory, in sorting and cataloging and shelving the mass of records that kept landing in the cramped back room of Louis' store. Trey was never sure where they came from, but they appeared, in heaps and boxes, water stained and in plastic sleeves alike. Some bore the marks of estate sales, though he never knew Louis to crawl any, and some where just boxes that could have contained a litter of kittens dumped on the side of a highway and to be collected by a good Samaritan.

Whatever they were and wherever they came from, Trey entered them into a spreadsheet on an ancient computer, stacked them according to condition and by rarity, as decided by a coffee-ringed binder kept on Louis' little-used desk, and then priced them accordingly. Then he carried the stacks into the store and slipped them into bins for sales.

Sales were not where the store excelled; Trey could generally count on one hand the number of customers they got on a daily basis: usually tourists, and the occasional hardened music buff, who kept the little hole of a store a secret from his collector friends so he would never have to pay more, or fight for a vintage copy of an album from some musician Trey had never heard of.

He was generally silent ringing these people up, slipping the record into a paper bag with the store's name stamped on the side. Louis paid him in cash from the till, and that kept everything from getting sticky for the both of them. Louis shared his cigarettes, stinky old man things, and kept him out of the rain.

Trey smoked cigarettes compulsively and squinted more than he blinked. On the streets that wound down to the beach and his place of employment, he slinked along like a broken cat, still wearing the same old black coat and boots he'd arrived in, fidgeting with the cheap shell on a bit of twine he wore around his neck.

Ten in the morning always brought the girl, and he stopped at the lamppost at the far end of the promenade to wait for her. She was a spectacle in a sea of them, but the only one that Trey ever focused on. She moved in a blur of color and non-color and he squinted in her wake, tasting the salt air on his tongue.

Trey doubted Shane's story at first, looking down on the top of his head next to Louis' balding one — the girl on the beach, on the sand, how could her wheels spin? But he knew better than to think Shane was lying; he was one of those strange beings that seemed incapable of it, and you could tell just by the air around him. It was an uneasy thing, knowing this, but Trey did — Trey always knew.

It was why he could live with a drug dealer: he knew Dash was sending back most of his money to a crippled baby brother in Kansas. It was why he let Kevin take the couch for his bullshit deformities: he knew the guy couldn't fuck a girl with another man's dick. He knew these things and knew Shane was Levron and atoned for every lie since by going without.

Trey the soothsayer, he thought to himself, waiting for the girl's four o'clock showing, eyes watering and cigarette burning down to his knuckles. The scar of the pentagram he'd carved into the back of his hand shone pink as winter moved into spring. He'd carved it there the day that Louis found him and pieced him back together.

Louis and the girl, though completely different in every way, were the two ends of a string that kept Trey upright. That Shane had the ear of both of them could have made him jealous, but it did not: Trey didn't work that way. He simply wanted to be somewhere in the chain of things, a circuit on the board, buzzing with the same information and energy.

Shane did not come to the store daily, but Trey was patient.

The morning after Shane had talked to her, Trey stopped and bought orange Mexican sodas and bags of Bugles at the corner store, and stowed them in a basket under the counter. It was food that would keep. When Shane came in the next day, a little dusty and tired-looking, Trey passed one of the sodas to him and they sat, watching the boardwalk fill and crowd and expand, like a sponge slowly gathering water.

Trey was patient, and they talked little, about this or that record as he sorted them, about the strange bits of things that Shane was tasked with cleaning and putting into supply boxes: mostly record player parts, and stereo pieces, things no one needed any longer but, like the albums, came in on mysterious little waves, in need of a home, and they were the stewards.

At ten, they both paused, heads poised so that their gazes fell on the open front door, and when the blur of the girl on skates moved from one end of the big windows to the other, and out of sight, their eyes followed in kind, heads turning like cats following a light on the wall.

When Shane's head turned again, their gazes met, and he laughed a little uneasily. Trey smiled, and it was an awkward gesture, as he was an awkward person.

"Old Faithful," he said; his voice was low and high at

the same time, rough like sandpaper, the sound of someone recently punched in the throat, even as he avoided physical contact at all costs.

Shane was momentarily confused and then his gaze turned sheepish and he nodded.

"Smells better." Anyone else, it might have sounded like a boast, but Trey knew that from Shane, it was simply a statement of fact.

They stood in silence for a minute, and Trey went again: "You saw her without skates."

Shane reached up and scratched at the back of his head.

"Yeah. It was weird, almost," he said, after a beat; this was the most Trey had possibly ever heard him say at once. This, all told, was the most either of them had ever talked: a veritable babbling.

They moved to the stools that Louis kept behind the counter, always perfectly arranged. The old man was somewhere in the building, rattling around like a bag of bones, and that knowledge was comforting, even as he stayed out of sight.

Trey drew one foot up onto the seat of his stool and wrapped an arm around it, finally reaching for the basket and setting it on the counter between them. "I've never seen her without skates."

Shane looked between him and the bottles, room temperature now and, after a moment, picked his up again, rolling the glass against his palms. He didn't drink right away, and seemed to be reading the label until his voice rose up again.

"She didn't have any shoes with her, but I think she'd been out all night." It was a consideration he'd been taking quite seriously for the past two days now, hours of thinking about the girl broken up only by small fits of sleep that never really brought rest.

"Huh." Trey fingered a bag of Bugles. "But why down at the beach?"

"Why not?" Shane tried to sound more flippant than he felt. He gave Trey a small smile and then took a sip of the soda, staining the paler skin of his lips orange.

"Just... I have no idea where she goes." Trey sounded forlorn, and was.

"Maybe she lives under the pier." That was impossible, of course, but her aim, at the end of the four o'clock trip, always seemed to be that: that direction, racing the sunset.

"Maybe it's the ocean." Trey squinted at the front door. The ocean was, indeed, off in that direction, but far from them, blocked by the boardwalk and teeming masses, the park, the slope of sand, everything covered in a haze.

"Everyone's entitled to their secrets." Neither of them had realized Louis was standing at the base of the stairs, his eyes brighter than either of them remembered.

Trey slipped to the ground; his sneakers slapped dully when they connected with the floor. Past Shane, their gazes met and then Trey turned and disappeared into the back room once more.

The soda was too sugary for Shane, but he drank it. It seemed important, as though the bottom of the bottle would contain a cut-rate genie with all the answers.

CHAPTER SIX

Spring was not subtle in that part of California: one day the morning dawned warm, and that was that.

Close to the beach, it stayed temperate, but one only had to cross the boardwalk, past the buildings, and the heat set in, enveloping, humid along the canals.

Shane avoided the wealthy neighborhood away from the beach. He felt tied to the water, more so since seeing the girl there, maybe even more desperately as she only appeared on her skates, ten and four, for days following. He went down to the water's edge every morning now, almost in a fever, feeling his blood pulsing in his temples. He had a cup of coffee sunk in the sand and a pastry laid beside it, with some wild and weird hope in his chest that she would come again.

She didn't. And her head didn't turn right nor left as she skated by, as if on buttered wheels.

It wasn't on purpose that he wandered away from the beach, then. There was some sense of futile sadness resting in his chest as the days warmed, as the flowers at the shop on the corner got lusher, the colors obscene. There was a dejected sensation as he walked, dark and skinny and separate from everything around him, heart pumping blood, uselessly, around his body.

He ended up near the canals, and it was such a different world from his own, for a long moment, he didn't know how to act. He was almost straining to hear the inevitable police sirens that had to follow such a sighting: a black boy like the Loch Ness Monster, alien, foreign to his surroundings.

In the daylight, it had the same harshness as any other neighborhood in California, but the shimmer of the water gave the houses a sort of glitter and sparkle like Vegas might. He found himself taking off his boots and shoving them under the bow of a disused row boat and padding closer to the edge of the water. Canoes were dragged up on the mossy banks though he could see, down the way, small piers and stops where the water came right up to the brick enclosures of the houses' yards. The water was still as glass but for the occasional water bug that lit on the surface and, holding his breath, Shane could only barely hear the hum and thrum of traffic and tourists just blocks away.

The water was warmer there, but he did not venture further, crouching to dip his finger in the liquid though he'd bared his feet. Even there, the water seemed suspicious — maybe even more, false as it was.

"Hey!"

The voice came from far off, and right behind him at once. Shane startled, stumbling back so he landed on his butt, the damp earth seeping through the abused fabric almost instantly. He would be upset about that later, but, for the moment, he was feverishly scanning the canal for whatever neighbor had finally noticed his encroachment.

No one.

His gaze lit on something silvery on the other side of the canal, crouched behind a paddle boat, glossy fingers clutching at the side, hair a wild mess over her shoulders.

"What are you doing?" he demanded before he could think of something else to say.

Her eyes darted from side to side, and then her focus retuned to him. "What are you doing?" was her return, like an echo.

That was a better question, maybe. Maybe she lived there, and it was Shane sneaking around where he didn't belong.

"I've never really looked at them," he said, finally, shifting his legs closer and tucking his feet under him; his ass was already wet, there was nothing to do about that.

"The canals?" Again her gaze swept up and down the expanse of water and then — then — she smiled. It was the first smile he'd ever seen on her face, and it made his heart stop cold in his chest, painful and swollen.

"They're not really for... people like me," he finished, gesturing down at his long body, the jeans that were a permanent shade of grey, the frayed and stained hoodie.

She studied him from across the water. The sun glinted off it at crazy angles, moving stars in front of his eyes even as he squinted against the glare.

"You never come back here because you don't belong?" She sounded surprised by this, as if the words sounded strange in her own mouth.

"I guess you could put it that way," he agreed, scratching at the back of his neck, the sweat gathering there, making his fingertips sticky.

"Oh." Her fingers curled against the hard plastic of the paddle boat and, for a moment, he thought he glimpsed gloves on her hands, the usual, but in some kind of shimmering green.

They disappeared behind the boat. "Turn around," she commanded him.

There was no reason for him to obey, but he did anyway, shifting up on his knees, moving in the mud and moss, so that he was facing the house on the side of the canal. It was larger than anything he'd ever lived in, thousands of dollars of real estate filled with furniture that, from his vantage point, looked un-sat-upon, perfect and magazine ready. He counted his breaths, each one in and out, ten, and then twenty, and at thirty, he vowed to turn at fifty, sure he was being had, and at forty-two, he felt a tap on his shoulder.

With his knees on the ground, she stood above him like a sentry, more so than she had on the beach. He saw her feet were bare again, and the jeans she wore were soaked to the knees, clinging to her skin like a second layer. She was wearing a tank-top, blue, and gloves, but yellow, knit and odd against the wet of her skin.

"How'd you get across?" he asked, struggling to his feet, slipping in the moss.

She looked over the water with a sort of casual disinterest, even as her hand shot out to catch his arm and bring him up to his full height, taller than her, but only just.

"I just did." Once he was standing, her hand dropped again against her side. In the later daylight, she was not so much silver as golden, the light shifting over her skin like it did the water, turning her eyes dark and then light.

"Were you swimming?" he asked, realizing that he'd not seen the straps of her tank top when she crouched behind the paddle boat.

She looked startled, but then shrugged.

"Yeah. It's calmer here. Fewer people. No one. Not till you."

"I was just walking," he replied immediately, somewhat defensive, and she stepped back, heels on the edge of the canal. He didn't know if it was a steep drop off, but his hand reached for her anyway.

Shane had not reached for anyone in some time. Initiating touch was not something he'd ever been good with, outside his mother, and certainly not out on the street. She lifted her arm up and out of the way and he knew, of course, that she was not too much unlike him, not really.

"You live out here?" he asked. There were some small pedestrian bridges, but, he supposed, someone enterprising could stow away under them. It seemed cold and dank, though, even compared to where he holed up.

She tugged at a long lock of hair, twisted and wet and gnarled, like tangles of seaweed. "Not really. I just like it here. Not a lot of people, like I said." Her voice was higher pitched than he remembered from the morning on the beach, but just as painful, rough and sweet at once.

"What about your skates?" It was as though everything he'd always wanted to ask her was rushing to come out at once and he was helpless under the force of its need.

Her eyes went to her feet: the nails were blue, round and perfect, each toe gripping at the moss like fingers. "Not on," she said, but when she looked up, met his eyes, she was smiling.

"Got me there." His hand was still reaching for her, inexplicably, and he dropped it next to his body, curling the fingers in towards the palm.

"I don't wear them swimming, Shane." Her eyes lit up and she clapped a hand over her mouth but, even with the fingers and glove covering it, he could see her smile.

"You know my name?" He was breathless, and gleeful, and his palms turned in her direction.

"I must have heard it somewhere," she decided, dropping her hand, letting him have the full effect of her smile on her heart-shaped face. Her chin was sharp and pointed, ears high on either side of her head. She was not what anyone would call beautiful, but there was something in her face that touched something deep inside of him, so deep, it felt a little like a knife wound opening up in his chest.

His hand went to the back of his neck once more. "Doesn't seem fair, you know," he said, eyebrows raised, eyes searching. "I don't know yours."

Her smile was wide, each tooth a shining white pearl. "Maya. You can call me that."

"Maya," he repeated, letting the letters roll, individually, around on his tongue. She didn't look like a Maya, not someone high-speed on skates, hiding out in a canal, walking the beaches alone at dawn.

"You can call me that," she echoed, pulling once more on the lock, rising up on her toes so they were the same height, eyes meeting: his dark brown, hers some indescribable color, more value than hue.

"What does that mean? Is it your real name, then?" he asked, suddenly confused.

Two salty fingers landed on his mouth, and her gaze glued itself to his. "It means that's what you can call me. Maya. If you need me."

She didn't give him time to react to that — why would he need to call her? She deftly stepped around him, smooth like she was on her skates, taking her fingers with her, feet silent as she scrambled up the incline and hopped over the fence of the house, through the garden, and right out of view.

CHAPTER SEVEN

When first dug, there were sixteen miles of canals in Venice Beach. By the time the twenty-first century had settled over California, only six remained, bordered by a neighborhood of multi-million dollar homes and dotted with bridges of varying characteristics, arcing pieces of art.

Shane walked the public path with an eye on the water. At some point, the majority of the canals had been filled in, due to stagnant water, or to make way for roads. Cars were fundamentally more efficient than boats, at least in a state where the town was not slowly sinking.

There was something sad about that, he thought, and he might have been studiously avoiding looking for Maya as he walked, choosing instead to contemplate the slow crunch of practicality over whimsy.

Venice had appealed to him, years ago, because a person like him would simply be another body taking up space. The same could have been said for New York, maybe, but there was an air of distraction when it came to Venice Beach: where the eye couldn't help but wander, the attention couldn't help but bounce from face to fire to skin to sea.

There was a safety in that chaos. The canals, maybe, were more wrong for Shane because of their orderliness than because they were rich and he was not.

Why had Maya run? He stopped at one of the ornate

little bridges and finally raised his eyes from the still water to the row of houses. She had given him a name now—Maya – and there was a sense of possession in that, as he turned it over and over in his mouth like candy.

Maya. It was awkward like a pebble, too round and sharp at the edges at once. He wanted to say it aloud, yet had no one to say it to.

Why Trey entered his mind, he didn't know. But he did, together with orange soda and the dank smell of the dust from hundreds of different homes that was carried in on the groves of the records, even as he stood under the relentless spring sunshine. Trey would know what to make of it. Trey would listen to the word. Maya.

Trey wasn't at the shop when he got there, though. Louis was, and Louis seemed to only care about Maya insofar as he was interested in her ass, tight from skating.. Despite this, he was someone, one of the only someones Shane could even speak to out loud.

"Maya," he breathed out, in lieu of a greeting, and the old man, smoking something fragrant that was not a cigarette put it out.

"What now?" His hair was unwashed, and clinging to his scalp. He looked harder than Shane had ever seen him, glinting and steely.

"Maya. The girl on skates. Her name is Maya." Each time he said it, the name, it sounded stranger to him, as though he were speaking a language long dead to human ears.

Louis ground the cigarette butt hard, crushing the paper and leaves inside.

"Might be that it is," he said, and his voice sounded like gravel, like flint, hard and harmful. "And now you can move the fuck on."

CHAPTER EIGHT

Maya was not her name, but she answered to it easily enough. Standing on the outcropping of rocks, she almost lost the sound of his voice, but it did summon her from the edge, and it had for as long as she could remember.

Venice Beach was an easy enough place to blend in. She never would have thought of it herself, but the boardwalk, just yards from the ocean, was as close to safety as she could imagine.

The skates she wore were white boots, with rainbow laces, pulled tight, double-knotted, held down at the top by an overlap of Velcro, squeezing her ankles upright. The wheels were pink, grey, and pebbled where they rolled along the concrete. She could feel every bump on the walk, where it gave to wood, to brick, and she liked it that way.

She watched the serious exercisers on their rollerblades, and knew that she could not stand the ride. There was a cushion of air around them, and Maya had a need to stay rooted even as she soared, slipped and slid through the crowds, light as air, smooth as silk.

There were dancers and puppeteers and fire-breathers and a guy on a unicycle who juggled knives. Maya was nearly six feet tall on her skates, yet whatever attention she garnered, weaving along the boardwalk, was forgotten in the melee of the rest of the freaks of humanity.

Shane and Trey and Louis were not the only ones who

watched her. In an obscure corner of the internet, there was a website dedicated to her, the Venice Skater Chick. This particular website garnered about ten hits a week. Tourists moved to take photos and rarely caught her. She was watched, for a moment, and then attention moved. But for Shane and Trey and Louis, no one would remember her if she didn't make her ten and four rounds.

She knew they watched. It was a curious thing, to know you were being watched. She could, if she turned her head to the left, meet their gaze directly even, a sixth sense even as she blew past in a blur. They were always there: Trey in the doorway of the record shop, Louis in the depths, Shane at his side or from the corner or down on the beach.

To say she was avoiding Shane would be correct, and not. That night on the beach so long ago had been an anomaly, a slip in protocol, the rules and regulations that bore down on her shoulders even as she pretended they did not. Even now, she paced her days so that he could not step in her path, but since she broke that under the light of the moon, she couldn't seem to shake him.

And so it was his voice that called her back from the tide, and from the creeping night, and she slipped into the shadows as easily as she did the crowds during the day. He did not know her name then, scrawny kid from the boondocks, just days at the beach, already a target. It had been on the tip of her tongue, before she could talk, even, to warn him, to tell him to look straight ahead, to turn his lips down, to stop fondling the key on the strap around his neck. He could have just painted a bulls-eye on his shirt and gone that way.

It was a whisper more than a scream that brought her from her perch, scuttling over the rocks like a crab, down into the carnage that was the unforgiving life of street kids. She always felt a sort of sympathy for them, lost inside a world that seemed determined to forget them, but they scared her, too: snarling like rats, tight fists and tiny eyes, feeding on the scent of fear.

She would never know where the courage came from. With the silver light of the moon and the black of blood, the sound was suddenly beyond hearing, beyond comprehension: felt rather than heard, flash of bright like the light of day, like a knife taken swiftly to the softness of the eyes. They scattered, terrified, and she finally padded forward, so light on the sand that she barely left an impression, naked and pebbled in the moonlight to crouch by his side.

He was unconscious, though she didn't know if it was the blows to the face — he was purpled around the eyes, and bleeding — or her cry that had done it. It mattered little: she dragged him up the beach with strong arms, to the open part of the sand, and hid at the rocks as the flashlight arcs made their way down to illuminate him, sprawled, bleeding, but breathing.

It was a mistake, and she knew it. Her fingers curled in her hair and her knees, bony, pressed to her chest as it trembled with each breath, more labored than the last. That she crept up after him just proved it. This would be the one she saved.

***

On each hand she pulled on the fingerless gloves. She tied the skates with those in place, legs covered by jeans, stomach and breasts by the tank top that stuck to her like skin. Maya fastened each piece to her like armor, rose to her feet like a giraffe first testing its legs, before she found her balance and rolled forward, picking up speed down the first slope that led towards the main part of Venice Beach.

It was comfort as much as it was a way to move: the wind on her skin and that rumble of wheels over the sidewalk. She never fell, but she suspected she would welcome that, as well, the connection to the earth, like a ribbon keeping her from breaking free entirely.

She never timed herself, but it was ten every morning when she appeared at the end of the boardwalk. The air was not too warm yet, and so maybe that was it: it still smelled salty from the ocean tide, the concrete holding the chill of the night. She could see herself at those times, like a bird, and she raised her hands just once, a wave to those she went past and never spoke to.

There was much speculation about what she did in the hours between ten and four, between four and ten, and the truth was: not a whole lot. She skated into the city sometimes, and back, but she couldn't make herself move too far from the ocean at any time. She tried, a little bit at a time, like a child trying out steps away from her mother's hands, but there was a pull that brought her in sight of the water, and her lungs always ached for the salty air, the wind that brought it in off the white caps. The city was full of smoke and harsh noises and grimacing faces, and though there were things she tried to see, to stare at, stand in, her feet always found her home.

Home was Venice. She skated over the little ornate bridges over the canals, up and down the streets of expensive houses and cars, past the flowers and leaning trees and smartly-dressed children.

And sometimes she did take the skates off. She stashed them in rental lockers and under abandoned stairs, in gardens no one was currently tending, and she let her feet meet the earth: the scalding surface of blacktop and the cool of grass, the grit of sand. She only did this when no one was around, when her hands were her own and her body was unnoticed.

Only Shane had glimpsed her this way. She knew why, and she didn't, and why she didn't rush away at first glimpse.

She simply couldn't.

She watched Shane, and the other boy, Trey. Maya liked Trey. He had a soft face, and tragic eyes, and a mouth that turned in an upside down smile, as though dragged down by two invisible little weights tucked in the pockets of his black carpenter jeans. She understood him, and wanted to touch his doughy skin, pet the hair that hung in his eyes like a protective curtain. Trey saw the things she did, and that pain — that was easy to feel sympathy for.

Louis scared her. There was no reason and there was every: he always seemed, to her, to be armed with a harpoon and bad aim, and that was the only reason she was still alive. He watched her, but not the way the other two did. His eyes were harsh, bottomless, colorless, and she shivered to think of his gaze close up. She never approached the store.

Trey had been chasing her since he arrived in Venice, and she let him. Of course, she could have prevented it, quite easily, but he got closer and closer and, at some point, he would catch her. Only for a moment, though: Maya was slippery like a fish, and there was rarely anything left behind.

She bathed in the canals. It was a strange place, maybe, but she could sink to her knees and feel the moss under her fingers, slick and alive and unmoving, and, at night, sometimes, she lay back and let the little rivulets carry her closer to the beach, and out of sight.

Rarely Maya spoke. There seemed little reason for it, and all of the people who caught sight of her always seemed to provide the words for her. She welcomed that, tasting the sounds of them, the saltiness of a consonant, the smooth butter of a vowel. She assigned each letter a color and let the words mix them. She spat out pain and hurt and mess, filled up on flower and sky and want.

She lifted comic books and little baggies of gummi bears, and, at night let boys with long eyelashes and water-bleached hair buy her drinks at a loud bar at the end of the boardwalk. The drinks burned but made her blood sing, and she danced, and let them touch her, but never peel away her jeans, or hold her hands.

Mornings were hard. And maybe that was the main reason she did not don her wheels for hours, and walked the beach, out of sight, until the sun was high in the sky.

Not now. Not anymore. Shane waited for her every morning and she watched him, from those same rocks, biting into her skin, waiting for him to give up.

CHAPTER NINE

"I swear it was here," Shane said, as he did every morning, and Trey appeared to believe him, nodded and gave one of his watery smiles, his expression as soft and unformed as a wad of dough. Shane felt like a fraud, biting at his fingertips, forgetting his coffee.

They went to sit at the spot Shane had been manning for more than a week now, nearing on two. He could find it with his eyes closed, feet sinking into the sand with every step.

What was it about Maya that had turned him into this? It felt as though it had been creeping through his veins for these years since he first saw her under the streetlight, like a dormant disease, and now he was in the middle of a full-on infection, a fever he couldn't cool down, a tightness in his chest that he couldn't loosen.

The dreams were more intense now, and he thought he could smell her in them. He was sure she had the scent of the ocean, far out and deep down, that cold and salt taste that was thinner and more polluted the closer the water got to land. She was pure, and distant, and he smelled her in those dreams, even as he could never breathe, woke up gasping for air and clawing out of the doorway in which he'd recently come to situate himself as the nights got shorter, and warmer, and the alleys scented rotting near the dumpsters.

"I believe you," Trey said, finally, and Shane shot him an uncomfortable smile. They didn't talk, sat, and eventually Trey pulled himself to his feet to move up the beach to the store.

Louis did not appear until nearly noon. Rarely had a customer ventured in before he arrived, and they hardly ever came in after. Trey did inventory, stowed and sorted and stacked, moving the contents of this bin to this bin, and though nothing ever really looked all that different, Trey could feel the movement in his limbs. He could sort stacks with his fingertips, the alphabet slowly taking hold where Donovan, years before, had organized the whole damned store by his favorite albums to his least. Trey had been resorting nearly since the day he started, marveling at the singular insanity that had to have been behind that organizational method.

As it was, no one really knew what happened to Donovan. Louis never brought him up.

Now the ABBA records were near the front of the store, and Trey lingered there at ten, and found reason to smoke a cigarette out in front of the store at four.

Trey did believe Shane, and understood the intensity of the obsession, too. The beach felt alive, humming with an energy that hadn't been there before, buzzing alongside the usual strange electricity of freaks and weirdoes and forgotten sacks of flesh. Trey watched for the blur that was Maya, and thought of Shane.

She'd not appeared before Louis barked in his direction, something like his name. There was a moment of confusion, when Trey looked between his smoke and into the store, darker, inky, with his eyes accustomed to the bright white of the sand. Finally, with a sigh, he dropped the cigarette to the ground and rubbed it out with the toe of his boot and worked his way back into the store, carefully, waiting for his eyes to adjust again.

He could almost feel the girl-- Maya, Shane called her,

though it sounded like the wrong name to him-- flutter by, like a humming bird, like a heartbeat. He stood in front of the cash register where Louis sat, on his strange, sagging throne, greyed hair pulled back in a ponytail that trailed over the faded plaid of his shirt collar.

"You talked to Shane?" His eyes were brighter than Trey thought he'd ever seen them, and they were sharp, making him shift back and forth from heel to the narrow sides of his feet.

"Yeah, a lil." Trey's voice always sounded choked, like he had a perpetual cold; coupled with his runny nose and blood-shot eyes, he looked it too.

Louis made a noise at the back of his own throat. "I didn't mean to scare him off." He did sound sorry, and Trey looked up through his fringe of hair, trying to study the old man's expression without looking it. Shane had not told him what Louis had said to him, but he could read it on both their faces, a sort of braille that his eyes traced instead of his fingertips. There was Maya, again, like a beat of a heart, like the incessant tapping of Louis' fingers on the countertop.

Louis noticed Trey watching him anyway. "I'm not a monster, Trey, you know that." Maybe it was supposed to be a joke, but he sounded weary, and he raised a hand to rub at his forehead.

"You tell him." He stopped, and he rolled his head back on his neck, eyes directed at the ceiling; he rolled his chin down to his chest, eyes directed on his knees. Trey waited, and listened to the sounds of the old man's body: the pop of his spine, the creak of his knees. He did not wonder about age, about how it felt to be old. He already knew that was not his future, not in the cards, and, maybe, that was why he was so willing to stand there, to wait, wait for Louis to speak, wait for the girl to skate by, wait for evidence of Shane's luck.

"You tell him," Louis began again, voice drifting towards the denim, the leather thongs on his feet, the cracked linoleum beneath. Trey shifted on his feet, and thought of Maya outside, of Shane under a tree with his eyes parched watching for her.

"He really should come back," Louis said, finally.

Trey didn't know quite how to respond. He'd been slipping Shane cash, money from the old pickle jar, money that appeared there as if by magic. He couldn't believe Louis knew, but he also couldn't believe he didn't.

Trey could feel his feet sliding on sweat deep inside his boots; he knew that was where Shane kept the cash, folded and tucked under his sole. He could feel Shane everywhere on his body, all of a sudden.

Finally: "I don't think that would work."

Always the soothsayer, always the truth-teller. Louis sighed and nodded. "Shame," he said, and when his gaze finally rose, it locked back on the ocean, down over the white of the beach, and he didn't say anything else after that.

CHAPTER TEN

In the end, he was the one to track her down, not the other way around. This would be important to her, that conviction that she'd done nothing wrong, that it was bound to happen, as he told her. That the sacrifice was made before she even knew there was one to be made, that it was a freight train and she was but one very small pebble on the tracks.

Trey did not meet Shane the next morning, and while Shane was vaguely concerned, it was on the level of being concerned about a cloudy day. He didn't know Trey well enough to worry about his safety, or really worry at all: he was usually there, but wasn't, and so he sat on the beach alone, sans coffee, and did not see Maya.

This was, of course, because Trey had found her the night before.

He had and he hadn't gone out seeking her. Once he closed the store down with Louis, who stayed silent the rest of the afternoon, he walked out of the door with his shoulders hunched and eyes on the pavement. He felt as though he were suddenly carrying a lot more weight than he had been to begin with — which was, all told, more than most people.

Trey could see the truth, after all. And when the truth came to you in the form of your own demise, it was hard to shrug off.

He walked the length of the boardwalk, to the big pier, the arcade there, the massive Ferris wheel that forever rotated up into the heavens and back down to earth. He sat at the end, under the scopes, watching the water lap at the posts. When night fell, he got up and walked again, up and down the canals, until he ended up in a brightly lit club, strobes flashing and girls sweating on the dance floor. He was, truly, utterly unsurprised when Maya appeared there in the center, somehow made of something other than skin and blood: composed of glitter and sinew and something untouchable, like every dream he'd had as a teenager, waking up in a suspicious puddle on his sheets and a sinking sensation of shame.

He followed her to the bar when she took a break, and she took an offered drink: pink over ice, an umbrella festooned with a wedge of pineapple and a poisonously red maraschino cherry. He could smell the vodka when she turned, sense her fingers tense on the glass when she met his eyes.

She was pretty and she was not, close up. He tried to smile and failed.

"You're Trey, aren't you?" Where she should have had to shout over the thumping bass, she did not, and he heard her perfectly.

He nodded, and held out his hand, flat, to her, palm pale and sweaty. She hesitated and took it, leaving her half a drink on the surface of the bar, letting him lead her through the crowd and out into the sharp night air.

He didn't kiss her, but she kissed him. It was desperate and sad and scared, and he tasted of tobacco and something peppery, sadness and something like courage in the form of spit and breath mints. Her fingers curled under the fabric of his shirt, against the give of skin and fat, hooked into the waistband of his jeans and under the elastic of the boxers that were never laundered as often as they should have been.

The brick of the building was rough even through his jacket, and her lips were chapped; when he pushed her away — gently — they felt burned.

She had tears in her eyes. "Why?" she demanded, with a little stamp of her foot on the cracked asphalt beneath them.

Trey shrugged, but, the truth was: he felt calm for the first time in his entire life. Where the weight had nearly pressed him to the ground that afternoon, that evening, his entire life, now there was a sense of lightness so powerful, he almost expected to take flight, grow wings from his back and be lifted right off the pavement and up past the lights that blotted out the stars.

"I won't." She tried to sound petulant, but was incapable. She curled her fingers into the thick locks of hair that draped down over her shoulders and back, tight, like ropes, until they turned purple, but still Trey would not answer

"You can't make me," she tried, pouting, backing up, right into the wall at the opposite side of the alley. They were trapped, both of them, and though what amounted to a staring contest began in that moment, and lasted nearly an hour, she did finally break down. She stood in place, pressing the heels of both hands against her mouth and crying quite freely until he offered her his hand again, no longer sweating, and they walked out of the alley, her feet moving more than dragging, but only just.

They walked to the water's edge, her flat feet, free of her skates, light on the sand, his booted ones sinking with every step. The ocean looked black and angry this late, and endless, and she whined against the wind, rising up on her toes and rolling back on her heels to avoid the water each time it slipped upshore. She would not get her feet wet.

"Are you sure this is what happens next?" she asked, voice soft, again, like in the club, but, this time, he did have to strain to hear her.

"I'm pretty sure," he said, smiling at her profile; she

was carved like a coin, and smoothed over by the same thumbs that would go seeking it in a pocket: distinct and not, like water.

"And then I'll be free?" she went on, drawing her shoulders to her ears, dropping them again. The motion clearly caused her pain.

"That's the idea." His voice was gentle, benevolent, and she finally looked over at him, eyes wide and shining in the half-light of the moon.

"That was your first kiss." It wasn't a question, and her chin quivered as she spoke the words.

Trey shrugged again, a light motion of his body, slowly loosing itself from the earth. "I like that it was you," he offered, squeezing her hand with his, the fabric of her gloves itchy against his palm. "Come on. It's time."

Maya whimpered again, but let him guide her to the water. It was cold against her calves, soaked the jeans she wore, but they kept stepping, hard against the waves, which rose before them, crashing down again just feet away.

"I don't want it to hurt," she told him, and her arms went around him.

He leaned his forehead against hers. "It won't." And he was the soothsayer, the truth-teller, and it wouldn't.

She nodded, kissed him again. And the water went silver where they sank under the surface.

CHAPTER ELEVEN

Shane waited in the morning, and the next, but by the end of the week, he just assumed the other guy had wandered off, and that was that.

There was a sense of loss, sure. Shane didn't have friends, really, and though Trey was strange and soft, and somewhat like the sand that sunk under his steps in the morning, he liked him, in a way. Trey was not threatening, or threatened, and there was something to be said for that.

He avoided the store. Some part of him knew that Louis would blame him if Trey had abandoned his post and, in a way, maybe he believed the same. There was something about the obsession for Maya that was slowly taking him over, like an infection, and maybe it was the same for Trey, or, at least, that was what Louis would think.

Shane still couldn't understand why Louis had suddenly turned on him. That afternoon in the store was so burned on his retinas that he could still see the hard line of Louis' mouth and the way he seemed to tower and blaze over him as he spoke, even when he blinked, even when he tried to sleep.

He strayed closer to the canals with a mounting paranoia, edging back to the boardwalk only to look out for Maya. She whizzed by, ten and four, and then Shane slunk back, looking over his shoulder for Louis, waiting for whatever it was that was going to follow him eventually.

The eventually did come, nearly a full week after Trey disappeared. But the eventually was not Louis. It was Maya.

She appeared in the same place on the canal where he'd found her before, popping up like a bird from behind a boat. That day, her eyes were wide and rimmed in red, fingers worrying at the flaking paint of the bow.

To say he was surprised was an understatement. Shane froze on the sidewalk, blinking several times, waiting for her to fade into some mirage that he'd brought up out of sheer memory.

But she was there, and she got to her feet, padding both further and closer, shaking a little.

"He didn't come back," she said, and Shane stared for a moment; surely a mirage didn't speak.

"Who?" he asked, finally, actually expecting the vision of her to break apart, float into the air like ashes from a fire, disappear into the sky.

"Trey." She lifted her hands, gloved, but the fabric was damp and dirty, the first time he'd seen them in that condition, in fact.

He turned to face her fully, sinking his hands into his pockets and pushing his fingers into his palms to make fists. He could feel a hangnail scrape painfully along the tender skin.

"You know where Trey went?" he asked, eyebrows drawing together. He felt weirdly offended.

Maya nodded, lowering her hands, digging her fingertips at the fabric of her jeans, as tight as ever, coated lightly with sand. Her shoulders curved up and in, her entire body almost creating a C-shape, a shell.

They were still standing on opposite banks, but the canals were so narrow, he thought he could probably take one, maybe two, steps, extend his hand and brush the fingers of her hand, should she stretch it out to him. She did not, however, and so he stayed where he was, clear of the water, hands tucked safely away.

"Where he is?" he asked, and she flinched with the sound of his voice. It was only then that he realized he couldn't hear the ever-present music from the beach, the drums and guitar and hum of people, and cars on the other streets. The only sound was the water lapping at the bricks along the edges of the canal, the boats floating on the water, green along the bottom with algae.

She didn't answer, her shoulders shaking with her breaths. Every part of her was dusty and dirty, and he eyed her critically. He was ready to threaten her — an odd feeling, as Shane rarely felt anger, and certainly not when it came to her   when she finally made a thin little coughing noise, more like a child than a woman.

"He went into the water. And he didn't come back." Her voice, too, was like that of a child, and when he focused on her face, she was chewing madly at her lower lip, sucking it in over her bottom teeth to grind the top set hard against the tender flesh.

"When?" He couldn't help it: he was barking at her, demanding and each time he made a noise, moved even a millimeter, her body jarred as if he were readying to strike her.

"A couple nights ago?" She sounded doubtful of her own reporting. "We went there and he didn't come back."

Shane's gaze swept up the canal, back, over her, up the other direction. They were the only people out, which had to be strange, wrong, uncommon: the canals were famous, and tourists posed on the little bridges to send photos back to their friends. It was, after all, the Venice of California, only lacking the gondolas.

"We?" he repeated.

She looked up with watery eyes; they were flat grey in color just then, and held no light behind them. "We," she echoed.

He turned away, stepped up and again to the lawn that bordered the sidewalk. In a flash, she was next to him, and he didn't have a chance to question that, to consider he'd heard not so much as a splash, as her hand went around his wrist and her grip was light yet iron-clad.

"He asked me to." She looked frightened, and spoke in a high whisper. Shane was quite sure he'd never seen anything quite as beautiful or quite as disturbing.

"What do you mean?" He didn't intend to sound suspicious, but he was. He felt trapped, even as she appeared made of bird bones, hollow, as though, despite her height, nearing his, he still very much could break her like a twig.

"I took him to the ocean and he didn't come back." Her voice was a whisper, choked like her throat was full of sand. He didn't know what to make of that more than he knew how to process what she was telling him.

"Does he know how to swim?" Some part of him always assumed that, because he couldn't, no one else could, or they'd all be in the water the way he wanted to be.

She raised her shoulders again, the points nearly brushing her earlobes, and stirring her masses of hair. "I don't think so."

He didn't think so, either: Trey didn't look as though he often shed his jeans and heavy black boots, and rarely washed his hair, or stepped into the sun. Trey was indoors, and shadows, and the water was far too exposed.

"So he went into the water and didn't come back?" Talking to her was like talking to a distracted kid, someone dumb, someone listening in on another line. She was all of those things, and it was growing maddening.

"Yeah." Her eyes flicked from his face and up the canal, the way his had, but did not return.

"You let him drown?" he asked, the magnitude of this dawning on him.

She made a pitiful sound. Shane wanted to seize her by the shoulders and shake her until her teeth rattled.

"Did you do something to him?" he asked, voice gone low and hoarse.

"No!" Her eyes were on him again, wide and stunned and clear and sharp. "I didn't do anything, I didn't kill him."

That wasn't even the question he'd asked, and her answer made his head swim. "But you took him out there," he said, balling his hands into fists in his pockets again. "And left him there. And he's not back and that kind of looks like you killed him." It did, and that was horrible, too much to envision.

"He asked me to!" Her hands moved in imitation of his, but fast, pumping like a pulse.

"But you could have said no." This was an insane conversation, and Shane felt dizzy, the sun too bright, white, smothering.

"You don't understand." Her voice was nearly a wail, and that was enough to do him in.

Shane stepped back from her, hand to his forehead, a tentative attempt to shade his eyes. But his head was already floating, and then his whole body was, and he thought for sure he saw fish dart by the edge of his vision just before everything went black, inky and dark and cool.

CHAPTER TWELVE

Wherever it was he woke up, he knew, quite instinctively, without opening his eyes, without inhaling a breath, that they were nowhere he'd been before.

This was confirmed once he sucked in a breath, opened his eyes. The air was dank, but salty, cold, and the sound of his inhale echoed off the craggy rocks that formed the cave over his head. His back was padded by damp sand, fine and soft, and there was a sort of constant lapping sound, a dripping sound, but very little light.

He blinked, and stirred, and cool little fingers landed on his face, his cheekbones and brows, pattering like rain. For a long moment, as he was slowly coming back into his body he was happy to let them.

"Where are we?" He knew, just as he had that he was somewhere new, that he was also not alone. He could hear another breath, shallow, and the fingers on his face where distinct and feminine.

The silence stretched and finally: "Somewhere safe."

"Maya?" His heart jumped, warm and beating in double time, blood surging through his veins, cushioning against the cold.

The fingertips paused, and then left his face. "Yeah?"

Shane struggled to sit up; for some reason, his entire body felt slack and heavy, as though his clothes had been soaked and turned fifty pounds heavier even as he knew they were dry. He felt her shift away, though there was little room to do so. The cave was narrow, and the overhead sloped sharply as it moved back, creating a darker black than at the front, where faint light filtered in.

"How did we get here?" He was sitting up now, rubbing his forehead, trying to avoid where her fingertips had touched, as though that might chase away the sensation.

"I brought you here." Her voice was as soft and spotty as her caress, as the sound of the water dripping against the rocks.

"Oh." That seemed reasonable enough, and he tipped his head back to gauge the height of the cave, brushing the back on a sharp rock.

He sucked in a hissing breath through his teeth and his hand went to the spot to find it damp. "Damn." It hurt in a way that was distracting, a small, sharp gouge to his scalp, making his fingers sticky.

Her presence neared again, and he could finally see her face when she moved into the watery blue shaft of light. She was silver again, like something from under the ocean, her movements just as much under the surface.

"You have to be careful in here," she informed him, hand cupping the back of his head. "It's not really big enough for more than one."

Of course that made him feel special, and he stayed still so she could examine his small wound with her curious little fingers, gentle even brushing over the small, jagged scrape.

"It's not too deep," she informed him, and regretfully withdrew her fingers. "It'll stop bleeding soon." He saw her wipe his blood on her jeans, as dirty as they already were, muddy at the knees.

"I wake up and bash up my head, awesome." He tried a smile. He truly didn't know how they'd gotten there, but the proximity of her body made him glad he'd done whatever it was to land them there.

"You're feeling okay now?" He couldn't read her voice, even as he went digging for some indication of happiness, relief, annoyance, anything, but it was inscrutable.

He nodded, touching his head once more; sure enough, the bleeding was already slowing, though the area was swollen and ached. "Did I pass out?"

He sensed more than saw her shake her head, the soft rustle of her long hair over her shoulders and shirt. "You just... needed to rest." It was an answer and it wasn't, but he couldn't really disagree with her: he knew he'd been exhausted, for days, and felt better in that little hole, despite the chill.

"Funny place for a nap." He wasn't good at joking, and felt the back of his neck burn. His attention turned to the front of the cave, where the faint shaft of light crept in.

"You ready to go?" she asked, and he glanced back in her direction.

"I-I guess so. How long we been here?"

Another silence, and she shifted up onto her feet, crouched low, her face fully in the triangle of light, blue and flickering. "Four days."

Shane startled, and looked towards the light, and back again. Her face was flat, even as her eyes were dark. Her features seemed as soft and changeable as buildings made of sand, and he had a desire to touch her face just to see if it might collapse.

Maya nodded. "Just crawl towards the light. I'll stay behind you. Only big enough for one," she reminded him, and the corners of her mouth twitched as though she might smile, but it never fell fully into place.

He nodded, and shifted onto his hands and knees. His muscles ached and, then, he could believe that it had been four days: he felt worn and heavy and atrophied. It was a bit difficult to get moving at first, the sand giving under his palms and knees and toes, fingers occasionally scraping on hidden rocks.

The cave sloped upwards, and it wasn't a long trek to the surface, through a hole at the top that was larger once he got there. He pushed himself up onto the outcropping, squinting against the white light of the sky, the reflection off the water.

They were on the beach, to be sure, and it took him another minute, two, to realize they were, inexplicably, on the rocks that ran along the beach front. They were located far down from the boardwalk, where the water broke violently, and where he was terrified to approach.

He scuttled back against one of the largest rocks, completely forgetting about the wound at the back of his head. Maya edged up next to him; her feet were bare, and dark with sand and cold.

"Don't worry." He could hear her voice easily despite the sound of the water smacking against the rocks. It was early in the day, so the tide was not high. Not yet. "We're safe here. I promise."

How did she know? He watched her profile for a second, as she resolutely looked forward, over the ocean, seemingly across hundreds of miles of white caps and the restless body of water that used its name to tantalize and trick.

"Is this where you live?" he asked, finally, rubbing his chin against his shoulder; only recently had he started having any need to shave, and four days in an underwater cavern seemed to be just about the length of time it took for this to be noticeable, the scruff sharp and rough.

Maya nodded without looking at him. Her hair was tangled down her back and sparkling with sand and the water droplets that clung to the strands, like diamonds precisely placed.

"In a cave?" He couldn't quite help but sound incredulous, as it was such a strange thing to discover. She was otherworldly, seemingly, of course, but this was like meeting a unicorn, or something similarly unbelievable.

She glanced over at him. Her eyes didn't look real, reflecting a color off the ocean that shouldn't have existed in nature, or, at least, not in waking reality.

"Where did you think I'd live?" She didn't sound judgmental, and not even quite curious, even as her strange eyes were searching his face.

His smile was hesitant, and crooked, shy. "I don't know," he admitted: for whatever reason, that had never been much of a consideration. "Maybe in one of those apartments that opens up to the roof. Like where you see the cages for the pigeons."

There was only one such building, and it was clear by the expression on her face Maya knew which one he was talking about. "I'm not much for the sky," she said, and dug her toes into the sand that filled the gaps between the rocks underfoot.

That hardly needed to be pointed out, and still he smiled. Shane ducked his head and looked back across the water. His heart rate picked up when he did so, the organ slamming at the back of his throat like it was trying to claw its way up, and out.

"You're more into the water, huh?" His face was cold with the spray that rose up with each roll of the waves, but it wasn't an entirely unpleasant feeling - even if he did feel vulnerable out there, conspicuous though their bodies were blocked from anyone on the beach by the height of the rocks, by their hunched postures.

"I guess." Her voice did almost disappear then, and she rested her chin on her dirty knees.

"I don't know how to swim," he found himself saying, and then pressed his shoulder to hers.

She pressed back. "It's okay," she promised, tipping her head just enough to look at him, ghost of a smile on her lips, silver-grey to match the waves, and the sky. "I won't let you get hurt."

Shane nodded, swallowing. There was something nagging at the back of his brain, something about that, but it wouldn't present itself fully: in it, he saw something like a face, limbs held in suspension as they drifted underwater.

"How long have you been here?" he asked instead, wanting to hear her voice as he groped for those unknowable answers, let his brain take that over while she spoke.

She licked at her lips, pink on grey. "I don't know," she said, after a moment. "A long time." Suddenly, she gave a sharp look in his direction. "How old do you think I am?"

"Fifteen?" he ventured. "Sixteen? I don't know. I'm seventeen," he offered, half in explanation, half in defense.

Maya gave a short nod. "I don't know," she repeated. "Years, probably. More."

He didn't know, exactly, what she meant by that, but he had also been on the street long enough to know that you didn't ask for clarification on that. Hell, he couldn't be so sure he knew exactly how long he'd been out there, either, as days tended to blur into one another, like fingers dragged over paint.

"Where are your skates?"

She looked confused for a moment, and then considered her bare feet, her toenails caked with dirt.

"I keep them somewhere else." And then, finally, a real smile. "Salt water isn't great for the wheels."

He had to respond with a smile, too. "Probably not."

They sat there, for several more minutes, and Shane supposed the sun moved through the sky, but the world around them was so bright and grey, he couldn't really tell.

"Tell me what happened to Trey," he said, voice muffled as his chin was tucked against his damp hoodie. Still, he could feel her stiffen next to him.

"I can't really do much but pass out again, right?" His own voice was wry to his ears, and her shoulders eased a little, by increments.

"You didn't pass out," she said, and he heard the slick sound of her teeth and tongue on her lips.

"I know." He didn't ask, though, what happened, didn't want additional confusion, or added anger — just some truths.

Maya nodded, and her fingers twisted into her toes. She was wearing her gloves, soiled and wet like a second skin over her own. "Trey," she began, in a hoarse little whisper, and had to clear her throat.

"Trey came and found me. He knew where I was, I don't know how." She seemed to be fighting to keep the defensive tone out of her voice, and, really, he could hardly blame her. "He came and got me and — and kissed me."

That wasn't the whole truth, and he could tell, but he didn't press, even if something like jealousy burned in his gut. "And then?" he prompted, instead.

Her fingers tugged at her feet, pulling them back so they were tipped up on her heels. "And he had me take him out to the water and let him go."

Shane nodded, watching the sea seem to react to her words, calming, pulling back, rising up and dashing some yards from their feet and sprinkling them both with cold droplets.

"He didn't know how to swim," he provided, a reminder, an urging to continue.

She shrugged in response. "I didn't want him to hurt and he said it wouldn't. And I kissed him and we went underwater. And when I came back up, he was gone."

"You just... let him go?" Again: he tried to keep emotion out of his voice, but it was hard, so hard.

"He wanted me to," she said, voice tiny and sharp, like broken glass. "He got pulled away. I couldn't hold on."

"Pulled away?" he had to echo, looking at her fully now, eyes wide.

There was a sheen of light over her, bright white, and she was dazzling, like sun off sand at mid-day, a mirage.

"Pulled away," she repeated, and though her voice was still broken glass, it was steady, the combination making her bottom lip tremble lightly. "I never would have been able to hold on, not anymore."

She had the skinniest arms he'd ever seen on anyone, including some of the scrawny little huffers by the pier. Still, they looked more like sinew, like ropes, than matchsticks, and he realized that she had to be telling the truth — other times, she could have held onto Trey, onto Shane, even, but something drew him away.

"Why did he do it?" he asked, after several minutes had passed. Suicide wasn't something he'd ever considered and, as such, it confused him and, really, scared the crap out of him. It wasn't like he really thought it was catching, but being so close to someone, physically, at least, for the week before, he and Trey, down on the beach, made him itchy and uncomfortable and worried about his own countenance.

Maya flexed her fingers but kept them laced up with her toes. "It was the thing that came next."

He didn't expect the swift movement that followed, though, her hands on both of his shoulders, fingers suddenly freed of their mates on her feet, the tips much harsher and sharper than he would have imagined.

"You can't do that," she said, eyes wide. Somehow, she was in front of him, beside him, all around him, and her eyes, wide and silver and gold and blue and green, filled his vision. "You can't let yourself go under. Do you hear me?"

Unable to do anything else, he nodded, once, twice, again. Her fingers dug into his skin, through his hoodie and shirt, kept him pinned there. Pinned, but not enough that he couldn't strain and crane his neck to close the distance between his mouth and hers, slamming them together with a shock, his teeth pressed suddenly into the soft flesh of his lips, hard enough to taste blood.

She made a sound, low, and moved to pull away, but then she was pressing back, hard, harder than he had, so hard both of their sets of lips parted. He could taste her tongue as well as his blood, and something deeper—salty like tears, but older. When his hands found her skin under her tight top, it was much colder than he expected.

Maya broke the kiss with a gasp, lurched away, collapsing immediately on the stand of rocks just a foot away. She looked precarious there, but something told him she would not fall.

"I'm sorry," he got out, but he felt strangled, and not sorry at all. She shook her head in kind.

"You need to go back." Her eyes cast up over the beach, scanning it from one end to the other, hunted, haunted. "I'll get you back. You trust me?" she asked, then, gaze back on him.

"Of course." What else could he say?

"Then close your eyes," she said, and, when he did, he felt her fingers on his temples, and the black of closed eyelids changed, smothering, a cool blanket, and then he felt nothing at all.

CHAPTER THIRTEEN

It wasn't four days this time, but it might as well have been. When Shane opened his eyes, it was dark, and Maya was gone.

He was safe, as she'd promised. He was tucked in a doorway that he didn't really recognize, as he'd never even attempted a squat there. It was, in a way, a prime spot, and so Shane, being as he was, and always on the tail end of an acceptable time to hunker down for the night, had never approached it. But there he was, that night, under a blanket that was dusted with sand, like stars, warmer than anything he had, but alone.

He shifted so his back was against the doorway and he could see the sky. The moon hung low, like a cup, and the lights of the city made it nearly impossible to see the stars. There was a hint of them, an indication, and one bright one in the bowl of the cresent moon, and he focused on that, the sound of the ocean dulled by the cap on his head.

Where had these things come from? The cave, what he could remember of it, was narrow, wet, cold, but the blanket was wool and did not smell of rot; the hat, either. She'd said she kept her skates somewhere else. Was there a house, one she didn't want him to know about? Why bother giving him the blanket and hat at all, then?

He pulled his hand out from under the blanket to rub at his eyes. It had been morning when she touched his

71

face, he was sure of that. With each passing moment, what he thought he knew slowly faded, dissolving like sand piles under the tide.

His fingers were warm. In fact, it was the first time he'd felt warm at night in years, and he felt conspicuous for it. Eyes rubbed, he slowly got to his feet, bracing his shoulder against the door as he rose, until he bumped into the door handle, then rolled to his other shoulder to continue.

His body felt heavy, worn, but not in pain. Back pressed to the plate glass, he stood there, watching the sodium-colored light of the streetlamp flicker in a circle over the pavement, the tufts of grass at the edge waving in a slight breeze. Night on the beach was chilly, even as the days could be roasting out on the sand, and when he tucked his hands into the kangaroo pouch at the front of his hoodie, his fingers touched a box.

He withdrew the package. It was cookies, chocolate; a brand he remembered from back home, but had not seen in California once. He turned it over in his hands, fingertips dragging along the edges, smooth and straight, the corners almost dagger sharp. He knew how they would taste, how they would smell once he ripped the cardboard flap, after he popped the shiny bag inside.

They had to be from Maya. All of it did. Why? Shane squinted and tried to remember their conversation, but it was blurry, muted as though he'd been wearing headphones on static and could only see the shape of her mouth, the color of her eyes.

The water spray at the rocks was cold, and though he was warm now, he could feel the sharp prickle on his cheeks. Had she killed Trey? Did he care?

He waited for the guilt of that thought to bite at the back of his neck but it didn't. Shane put the package of cookies back in his pocket and rested his fingers on them, staring out over the boardwalk.

He formed fleeting plans to look for Maya in the

morning, but when it dawned, bright and sunny to the point of glaring distraction, he knew he wouldn't. That they'd sat in a totally grey world when he first woke meant something, he was quite sure, and Maya, though she made those rounds on the boardwalk with regularity, was like a mirage on sunny days, appearing and disappearing just when your eyes managed to focus.

There was a grief in this, and he packed his bag, and the unopened package of cookies and the blanket, with slow movements. Despite his experience on the street, his hyper-vigilance that was simply necessary to survive, he was wholly in his own world. When the shadow fell over him, he'd not even heard an approach. Indeed, it took him another moment, two, to even look up.

He knew it wouldn't be Maya, but the hope was there anyway. It was Louis.

Shane froze. There was no reason to believe that Louis would hurt him, but, since he'd left the store that day, and Trey's silence on the matter — and Trey's disappearance, too — Shane had cultivated a fear of the old man that loomed, dark and growling, in the relative darkness of the doorway.

Louis was holding coffee, two cups. It smelled incredible, like warmth and comfort.

"Come on, kid." His voice sounded like gravel was stuck in his throat, and, once Shane's eyes managed to climb to the other man's face, focus, he realized that Louis was haggard, grey and tired-looking.

Shane straightened up, pulling the bag up to his chest rather than his back. He had some internal need to keep his distance, to pad it between them, and Louis took a step back as he did so.

"Where are we going?" he thought to ask, even as it was a stupid question and Louis reacted as such.

"The moon. Where do you think?" His voice was humorless, and weary, and Shane was too surprised not to follow him out of the doorway and down the street.

At the door to the record shop, Louis handed him one of the cups of coffee, and fished his keys from his pocket. It was several false tries at the lock, cursing under his breath, before the lock gave and he pushed the old door in. It swelled and shrank in the salty ocean air, and was cracked and splintered all along the edges. Shane caught the frame with the fingertips of the hand holding the coffee after Louis stepped in ahead of him.

"Come on," the man insisted, though there wasn't really exasperation in his voice where Shane expected it. He looked up at the rafters of the place, where dust danced in the lights that were starting dim, warming up after a night off. "Getting dusty up there," he noted, and it came out so incidentally, Shane almost missed it. Then, of course, he remembered that Trey did the bulk of the work in the store, the sorting and moving and dusting, and he understood.

He stayed in front of the door, though he had let go of it, and it settled against the frame, unable to shut without a good shove. "What do you need me for?" he asked, in the most measured voice he could manage, though there was a sudden panic at the back of his throat. It was disconcerting and made him feel silly, and small.

Louis was settling behind the counter, up on his stool. His jeans were dirty, but they were always in that state. His hair was pulled back in a ponytail, but the top was rough, strands broken and standing up and hanging over his forehead.

"Shane." His voice was louder now, and steadier, and Shane swallowed, finally creeping up to the counter to put his bag down. He did not go to the stool that seemed to still be waiting there for him. Instead, he set his coffee down on the glass surface and leaned against it, suddenly wishing he'd kept the cookies in his pocket and could open them now, dunk them in the hot liquid to make the chocolate melt. Something about removing them from his pack now, in front of Louis, felt wrong, like he would be giving Maya away.

Louis watched him with one of those strange, flat grey eyes, the other seemed to look right on through him. "You think I'm gonna hurt you or something now? Real jumpy," he added, as if Shane needed the clarification.

He shrugged, turning the coffee on the counter with the fingers of both hands. Part of him said certainly not, that Louis had actually taken care of him, and likely ensured his survival time and again, but the way he'd looked when he told her to avoid Maya — and that he'd done the exact opposite — told him that Louis couldn't be trusted, as much as no one out there on the street could be, even in the confines of a store. That security was all the more false.

A sigh escaped Louis' lips and he shook his head as he reached for the coffee, lifting the cup to his lips.

"I just want to know where Trey is, Shane," he said. Now his eyes were definitely looking past Shane, over his head and out the plate glass windows, smudged, and towards the ocean.

The boardwalk was empty that early in the day, and it struck Shane that he'd never seen Louis up this early. Trey opened, always had, since Louis had taken him on, as far as Shane knew. Louis never came in before nine, and he was always bleary-eyed when he did so, dirty and surly, as though he'd been up most of the night, while the rest of the world slept like a bunch of suckers, or losers, depending on his mood.

Shane couldn't answer, ducking his head to look down through the small hole in the cup at the black liquid within. Trey was gone, he knew that. The story Maya had told him was murky already, faint and not altogether real-sounding in the light of the day, bright and sunny, a different world than the one he had inhabited with her out on the rocks.

He chewed at the corner of his lip and listened to Louis loose a pack of cigarettes from his jacket pocket, saw them as they dropped into his frame of vision there on the counter top, along with a lighter. He wanted one, badly, now, but did not reach for them.

"The kid couldn't swim, Shane," Louis said, finally, and his fingers dug out a crumpled and creased cigarette, which shed some of its tobacco as he rolled it up between his knuckles and it floated out of Shane's focus on the way to his mouth. He heard the hiss and crackle as it was lit.

"He wasn't supposed to die," was what came from Louis' mouth next and Shane found his gaze snapping upwards, only to lock with Louis'. Both of his eyes were focused now, steel grey: not accusing, but steady, waiting.

"Who's to say?" Shane's voice cracked, and he wished he was as brave every day as he was the day he pushed past the step-father and bolted from the apartment.

Of course, considering that bravery was tricky in itself.

He tried to steel his jaw, keep his chin steady, tipped up, but it was difficult against the way Louis was staring him down. He swallowed.

"Drowning's a hell of a way to die, Shane," Louis informed him, taking a long pull off the cigarette. The embers flared red, and burned their way along the paper, before he lifted it from his mouth and the thing went black and smoking.

"It's suffocating on an incredibly helpless level. You choke and smother at the same time," Louis intoned, and Shane felt his chest constrict.

"How do you know he drowned?" he asked, finally, voice hoarse and words difficult to get out.

"He always knew he would," Louis said, simply. "He told me that the day I met him, out on the sand. That he was going to drown and he was just there, wondering when."

Shane stared, openly, mouth drooping a little so that his breaths were coming nosily from between his lips. Had Trey ever said that? The two of them sat there on the beach for hours a day, waiting for Maya, and the other boy had never breathed a word about his fear, if there was one. Trey was a quiet person, was hard to read: was he afraid of death, or was the inevitability something comforting, like knowing the sun would come up in the morning?

Louis was watching him. "You see?" he asked, and Shane did: the man had taken care of the both of them — wasn't it his due to have the truth?

"She took him out there," Shane found himself saying. "Into the water. He asked her to."

"Do you believe that?" Louis' eyes had not left his, and Shane looked to the right and left, anywhere but at the old man, but couldn't quite keep his gaze from traveling right back to his craggy face.

"I do," he whispered, a swell of conviction in his chest, as small as it was. He believed Maya — and he believed Louis, too. Trey was going to die, and he knew he had to die, and he'd had Maya help him.

"Why would he ask to meet his death?" Louis pressed, his voice suddenly sharp.

Shane was able to hold his ground this time. "Because he knew it would get him in the end."

His gaze finally met and held Louis', as dark as the cave when he'd woken with Maya's fingers on his face. "You can't outrun death. Eventually — you just have to stop trying."

CHAPTER FOURTEEN

Louis had been standing at the water's edge for years.

He'd been a young man when he arrived in California, and now he was old. Forty years had passed in the meantime, and he felt every one of them, from the skin turned harsh and leathered in the sun, to his vision, spotty, hair greyed, and the rough rasp of his fingertips against the sand, now, rocks against rocks against rocks.

The sea was aching for him, and that was why he remained there, on the boardwalk, in sight of the beach, the rolling waves, the endless expanse of blue-green. It would claim him eventually, but he fought it in a way that he thought Trey should have fought, and the way he wanted Shane to fight, all of them passengers on the same boat.

The young man was more obstinate than he'd been as a youth, his first days on the beach, his years after buying the ramshackle shop, the inventory secondary to the location. His fingers skimmed over the spines of cardboard record sleeves, and though he knew the names and sounds of each of them, they were beings on a different plane than the one he existed upon. They were on plane of the living, the truly living, something other than the one inhabited by those haunted by the water.

He shook his head as Shane slipped out the door again. He would go after the girl, Louis knew that. Louis knew things that Shane wouldn't be able to fathom.

Louis knew the touch of that slippery sense, of fingers that felt forever dipped in something cool and silvery, salty, of eyes that never shed tears, and flanks covered and not. Her skin sparkled in a rainbow, her hair of some texture he could not find on land.

It was easy to believe that he didn't understand: surely Louis' brain was fried by a variety of drugs, by the sand and sun and surf itself. He had been a surfer before he landed there, his limp visible even then, the limp that took him out of the whole scene. Louis had been a young man once, and now he was old.

Trey had known this. Trey had seen things that no one thought he did, and he and Louis circled closer, and the old man gave him cigarettes and a place to duck out of the harsh sunlight and wait out the inevitable.

"The days are getting longer," Trey had noted, but a week, two earlier, just before he slipped out of view. He smoked in a nervous fashion, his fingers forever moving, and Louis could be distracted by the movement of his hands, like birds attached to his arms.

"Creeping closer to the solstice," Louis had remarked, idly, rolling his own joint, a point of distraction, a necessary medication against the days and nights.

Trey had shrugged, looked out the front door. "It feels like things are stretching out, though. Getting longer. Like I have to wait longer for a day to end."

The older man had considered him for a brief moment before turning his attention back to the hash and rolling papers on the glass counter before him. "Days and nights are always the same length. Otherwise, you know, shit would get complicated."

"Maybe it already has." Trey's voice rarely rose above a powdery whisper, but that shot across the store like a bullet loosed from a gun: high speed and dangerous, his aim true.

Louis had kept his head bent. He had never quite been able to look Trey in the eye, the young man entirely too perceptive, deadly.

"You really should get stoned more often," had been his reply.

Now Trey was gone. The boy had spoken of the inevitability of his demise, and Louis knew better than to argue with that. There was a loss in it, though, that dug deeper and clung harder than he would have expected it to. He was not a family man, after all, but he'd gone and collected these strays, Donovan and Trey and Shane, and each one of them drifted off, in one way or another, and it was the sea that he blamed, fairly or not.

He closed the store as Shane made his getaway. Hands in pockets, he made his way down the beach. The sun was up, but the air was still cool with the night it had banished, the sand retaining that chill, sinking under his feet. He'd not removed his sneakers, and they filled quickly, grating but grounding.

The rocks were far down the beach, and the slog through the sand made it a long walk. Louis kept a steady step, over and over, and the sun was starting to heat the beach by the time he reached them.

He'd not expected to find Shane there, but was just as unsurprised when he did. Shane, however, startled, and stumbled, and landed on his ass on the sand. Jumping quickly to his feet, he assumed what Louis knew to be a defensive stance, and he waved a hand irritably at him.

"I'm not here to hurt her," he informed the boy, but that information just made Shane narrow his eyes.

"How did you know this is where —" He faltered; did Maya actually live there? It was awfully cold, and wet, and, he reasoned, rather dangerous.

"I know a lot more than you give me credit for, kid," Louis grimaced, turning his face towards the ocean, watching the waves roll in.

"You think she's pretty, don't you?" Shane's voice

came from somewhere behind him, years younger, and it took Louis a moment to turn his attention there, wild eyebrows raised.

"What's that got to do with anything?"

Shane shrugged; he was something like sixteen years old, and Louis remembered being that age, and being swayed the same.

"Pretty or not," he said, after a moment.

"She didn't kill Trey," Shane said, in a soft voice, chin tucked against his chest.

"She took him out there," Louis countered, inclining his head towards the ocean.

"That isn't killing him."

"What would you call it?" Louis was irritated, but, moreover, was scared — scared that Shane was going to get himself killed, same as Trey, same as Donovan.

"Getting away." Shane's eyes were on the water now, and his breath rattled in his chest.

Louis couldn't quite reply to that, not for a moment, not for several moments, eyes back to roaming the crests of the waves. The Pacific was poorly named, but, in a way, aptly: he'd surfed those waters for what felt like centuries, and there was a sort of Zen-like calmness that settled in his blood and bones when out on the water.

That was back then, though. And now was a whole different ball of wax.

"Shane, where did you come from?" Louis shook his head almost immediately, and rubbed his hand over his hair, freeing a plethora of grey strands, sending them dancing in the glaring sunlight.

"Scratch that," he started over, looking at the boy. "Start with your name."

Shane's eyebrows went up, and they likely would have continued an upward trajectory had they not met the natural resistance of muscle, shooting pain through his forehead.

"Levron," he said, finally, shoving his hands in his pockets; whatever bluster he thought he'd had in him a minute before was suddenly gone.

"And you're a runaway, right?" It was a question that didn't really need asking: the majority of the kids that ended up in Venice Beach were there, almost to a person, because they'd run from something. Venice was like Wonderland, like Narnia, like every made-up land from an author's pen: far away, warm, exotic, full of characters that could exist nowhere else.

Shane's gaze was steadily dropping, down past Louis' belt, the line of the sand, to his sneakers. There, he gave a small nod.

"Everyone's running. Life's a race." Louis reached into his shirt pocket and got out his cigarettes, a faithful old friend. "It's a competition and not. What's getting dead faster than someone else going to do for you?"

Shane stayed quiet. Louis lit up his cigarette, sucked in the smoke and held it, lungs burning, before releasing it into the breeze, the tendrils swirling back towards his face.

"Running isn't always a movement, a forward motion," Louis went on, scratching his chin with the side of his ragged thumbnail. "Sometimes it doesn't look like movement at all."

"Are you running?" Shane found his voice, though his eyes were resolutely directed downward.

"Didn't I just say everyone is? To, from, whatever. Everyone runs." He pulled in another tar-coated breath. "I wasn't always old, you know."

Shane shrugged. "But you gotta stop sometime, don't you?" He chanced a glance up, dropped it immediately.

"Not really. Still running. Maybe in place, maybe in a small circle, maybe a step forward, dart back." He cast his cigarette away despite it only being half-smoked.

"This is my advice, Shane, Levron." Shane finally pulled his gaze up and almost had to support it with his hands, to keep it steady on Louis' face.

"Stay away from her." His voice was firm, though it was competing with the waves against the rocks for space in Shane's ears. "Go home. Go back where you came from. Running for the end can wait."

His breath felt strangled, forced down his throat at the idea of going back, of turning and heading on that road to a life he'd not allowed himself to think of since the day he left.

"And what if I don't?" Louis had no real power over him, but the ability to report him to the cops which Shane knew, instinctively, he would not.

"God help you, kid."

CHAPTER FIFTEEN

Maya only appeared when Louis was gone. One moment she was not there and then she was, watching the man's retreating back over the beach, the uneven gait of his limp and the sand, and she worried her hands in front of her, sliding the hemmed ends of the nubs of her gloves along the joints of her fingers.

"He told you to leave," she said, sort of in Shane's direction, but she did not turn towards him. He was left to watch her back, too, the way she was watching Louis', with a sort of concentration that made little sense.

Her shoulder blades were prominent, and they created wings, or the impression of them, under her shirt, as though folded and hidden until the time for flight. He wanted to touch them, run his fingertips along the hard edge, and he found his gut aching just staring at them.

Maya glanced over her shoulder, hair stirring. "He knows your real name. Aren't you scared?" Her silver eyes were wide as saucers.

Dragging his attention from her back — he was leering at it as most guys would her breasts — he shrugged.

"Why should I be?" The name wasn't important, and never really had been — it had been a whim, really, to rename himself, a rebirth if he was feeling generous, but, mostly, he'd just been unaware of how very little the cops cared, so long as he wasn't lifting or pickpocketing or huffing in the open.

She looked back to where Louis had gone; Shane couldn't really see him at that point, but Maya was squinting.

"Names are dangerous things," she breathed.

That annoyed Shane, and he dropped back onto the sand with a graceless movement, pushing his hands under the grains so that they were quickly turned grey and gritty. "Not everything is dangerous."

She made a humming sound and finally turned; her feet were bare, again, thin and long and dirty.

"I guess not," she said, but she was clearly doubtful. His fingers stirred the sand and, after a minute, she squatted down in front of him.

"You believe me."

Shane glanced up, still irritable. "Why wouldn't I?"

She let her eyes linger on his: of course he knew why he shouldn't believe her. The bizarreness of the story was foremost, and he could grudgingly agree that, maybe, he wanted to believe it, believe her.

"Why would you lie about it?" he said, this time, and she nodded at this far more acceptable answer.

"Well, you don't really know me, do you?" Her voice was softer now, and, he thought, sadder, strangely.

He wanted to touch her, more than he'd ever wanted to touch another person in his life.

"You can let me know you, if you want." He cringed at his own words: they sounded clumsy, stupid, and he bit his tongue until the pain crawled to the root.

Her fingers sank into the sand, to the gloves over her hands, the grains catching on the knit material. "Louis thinks you shouldn't."

"I don't care what Louis thinks!" he blurted, voice fierce, fierce enough to make her flinch.

She didn't draw back though, and pushed the tips of her fingers up through the surface of the sand without a response. Shane felt instantly bad, and tried again.

"Louis isn't a bad guy," he said, slowly, and she nodded. He was figuring out what she wanted to hear, though he couldn't, for the life of him, understand why, or why he was doing it.

"But... I don't think he's got it all together. In his head, I mean." Was that cruel? Was he making up a strawman to absolve himself of the idea that Louis might not be completely off his rocker?

Maya seemed to think so and she gave him a careful look. "You don't believe that."

"What am I supposed to believe, Maya?" Shane sighed, balling damp sand into his palm. "That you're both dangerous? That you're not? That Trey killed himself or that you killed him or — Louis knows you and what you do? Is that it?" The idea came quite suddenly, and his eyes were suddenly keen on her, in a way that did make her draw away this time.

"What do you mean?" she asked, softly, voice barely above a whisper.

"Trey knew he was going to die," Shane said, slowly, blinking with each word. "And Louis knew where you — where you live. Did... did he know that Trey would go to you?"

Maya fell silent, and it was fitful, her toes digging in the sand, eyes darting every which way in an effort not to connect to his gaze. Shane took in every movement, every flicker of muscle in her skinny shoulders and her fine-boned face, her expressions making an impact despite their fleeting nature.

"Do you know Louis, Maya?" he asked, after several minutes of that quiet, of the both of them sitting in those increasingly uncomfortable positions, his jeans starting to grow damp at the seat.

"Maybe." Her voice was merely a squeak, and certainly she still was not looking at him, pushing sand up under the edges of her gloves so that her hands were nearly buried to the wrists at that point.

"How?" Shane was rarely that pushy, and it felt strange on him, like he was donning someone else's skin, and they were shorter, smaller around the shoulders and chest, constricting his heart.

Her eyes finally met his, and they were wide, watery, pleading. "Please," she got out, word, as small and simple as it was, laced with a pain that he could feel as well.

"Maya, tell me." He was more commanding than he'd ever been in his life, and his eyes were dark and wide and hard on hers.

"A long time ago," she got out; her voice was high, thin, almost piercing, like a note on a tight string, a needle slipped under the skin.

"And?" It felt strange to be pressing like this, but it was as though he were poised at the top of a hill, gravity tilting him further and further forward, and nothing was going to stop the fall.

"He loved me," she said, teeth biting off the last word so it almost didn't escape her mouth. Her chin trembled as if she might cry, but her eyes did not well up with tears.

Louis was old. Maybe not so old that he should be dead, but he was so much older than Shane, it sounded gross to think of the man being in love with Maya. It seemed wrong, for a man more than twice his age to want a girl who looked even younger, with her smooth skin and face with rounded cheeks.

His mouth went dry. "How old are you?"

Her lips twisted like a string, and she pulled her mouth from right to left and back again.

"Old," she said, finally, lips sticking at first, popping apart, and she licked at them with the tip of her tongue. "I... I don't know exactly. Old. Much older than you think."

"Seventeen?" he attempted, with the faintest of laughs, so faint, it couldn't possibly count.

Her smile returned, for just an instant, flickering like a candle, and she shook her head. "Not in a long time."

This time, it was his gaze that dropped, almost frantically, down to the ground, to their fingers there, her toes buried, feet blue and cold-looking. He knew, again, she had to be telling the truth — why would she lie about that? It wasn't like he could tell anyone she was a minor, just as he was. She had no reason to weave a story like this, about Trey, about Louis, about her skates, her hide-out behind the rocks.

Finally, chin pressed almost painfully against his chest, he asked: "What are you?"

He could only hear her exhale, couldn't see the frown on her face, the way she gnawed at her lips, which were bright red from being worried against her teeth. Tucked so tightly into himself, he couldn't even see the way her shoulders rounded in his direction, the way her elbows lifted in desire to pull her hands from the sand and touch him.

"I don't think..." His body tensed and she made a clicking noise with her tongue before trying again: "I don't know that you'd believe me."

He let out a hollow laugh, pointed at his chest and the ground. "I've believed everything else, haven't I?"

The silence stretched again and, if he couldn't see her ankles from where he was sitting, he might have thought she made a getaway. Then her toes popped up through the sand again, blue, cold, and then her fingers.

"You're right." Her hands reached out to him, but, almost on instinct, he shrank away and she dropped them back to the ground. It was only for a moment, though, and she lifted them once more to peel the gloves away.

He expected nothing, and, so, was quite shocked at the reveal. Her hands, shaped like hands: small and square with long tapering fingers, were a shimmering green, covered in scales that ringed over her wrists and along the backs, fading only as they reached her knuckles. There was webbing between each, transparent and blue, stretched thin and veined delicately, silver and pink and orange and purple.

Shane sucked in a breath between his teeth. She held both hands out to him, turning them so he could see the smooth, pale underside, covered in smaller scales, like the belly of a fish. Her fingers flexed, and the scales rippled, the sunbeams bouncing off them like a disco ball.

"You…" He looked up, finally, to her eyes, silver and gold and green and blue and everything else, wide and patient and sad. He opened his mouth to try again, but failed.

"I've been coming to this beach since I was a child," she said, softly, glancing down at her hands, curling the fingers in towards her palms, the webbing fluttering and folding in as she did so. "Once I could, I climbed the rocks, and watched people. People — your people — you're…" She breathed out. "Wild animals, untamed, unaware of how fleeting your lives are, how little what you do matters. Like dynamite, contained, always about to explode, with no warning."

He was almost too distracted, watching her hands, to hear her words but, finally, he did lift his eyes back to study her face.

"My people?" he repeated, eyebrows raised. "What do you mean? You're… you're not like us?"

She spread her hands again, and shook her head. "I am, but I'm not. I can be," she added, voice immeasurably sad. "But I'm not. Not really, not totally."

"You have scales," he said, an observation that hardly needed to be made.

Maya nodded. "Scales, and gills and, sometimes, a tail." Her smile would have been playful if it wasn't so melancholy, pained. "Do you know what I am?"

"A mermaid," he breathed out, and she was nodding before the word had even finished passing over his lips.

She made a faint face, but was smiling again, this time with slightly more mirth in her expression. "That's such a silly word," she informed him.

He knew not to take offense, but there was something in him that did anyway. "What else am I supposed to call you?" Shane shook his head. "What do you call yourself? Your... kind?"

She shrugged, the sharp points of her shoulders looking more like fins to him with the new information. "We don't call ourselves anything. Not — not the way you name things. It's... different."

Of course he was instantly curious, of course there were dozens of questions crowding his mind, but none of them made them to his tongue. What did was: "I saw you, that night. When I first got here, when they beat me up."

She licked at her lips and looked down at her hands, the scales shimmering in the glaring light of the day. "Yes."

"You stopped them." He'd never thought of that, not until that very moment, and something stirred deep inside him, somewhere he was quite sure had never been accessed, or, at least, hadn't been in a long time.

"I did." Her voice was soft, bubbly, somehow like the sound of foam on the crests of the waves. "I... I didn't think it was fair."

"Did you do that for Trey?" Without meaning to, he was holding his breath.

Maya shook her head. "Trey was different."

"Louis?" he asked then, resisting the urge to rub at his forehead.

At that, she did nod, almost with chagrin, another sigh escaping her lips. "That was different too."

Shane found himself shaking his head, though there was a vague pulse of disappointment at the back of his skull. "I don't want to know," he said, honestly, and, finally lifted his fingers, brushing the back of her hand, where the scales were cool and smooth. "Just, you know, thanks."

She shivered, and looked up over his head. "Sure."

They were both silent for a long time, but Shane listened to his heart beat at his temples, counting the thuds in his skull, before he spoke again. "Why?"

"Why what?" She'd clearly been caught by surprise, and her hands spread briefly, the webbing flaring and then quickly folding back in.

"For, just, everything."

Her smile was sudden, surprised, genuine. She lifted one of those strange hands and cupped his cheek. "You're welcome."

And then he kissed her.

CHAPTER SIXTEEN

It was a kiss made up of waves crashing on a rocky shore, of the depths of the ocean, cold and black. It was a kiss colored green and blue and gold, of sunlight filtering through murky saltiness. It was a kiss that built sandcastles on the beach for the tide to eat away at, a kiss that could smooth like glass or whip into a frenzied storm. It changed his life with just the rapid pulse through his veins, and the sun beating down on his back.

They both gulped for air when they parted, Maya's usually silvery skin purpled and pinked, up over her cheeks and on the points of her ears peeking through her winding locks of hair. She lifted one of her strange hands to her lips and brushed the cool blue tips over them, her eyes bright and shining on his, gaze something unlike women he'd known, girls, without the same sort of bashfulness. She looked confused, and amazed, and her mouth turned up under her fingers, a smile that was wicked around the edges.

"That's not how you kissed me before," she said, still breathless.

His own smile was crooked, pleased, dazed as though he'd stood in the sun all day. "Didn't know I was kissing a mermaid then."

She laughed, and he was quite sure he'd never heard a sound like that before: it was something like videos he'd seen of dolphins, a strange sort of chatter, both painful and sweet. His fingers curled around hers as her hand dropped to the sand again.

"Do you still think I'm in danger? With you?" Shane chanced asking.

Maya bit at her lips, stained purple, pink, flushed deeply. "Probably," she said, softly, ducked her head, keeping her eyes on his. "I'm having trouble remembering why."

"You've told me the truth now," he pointed out, and, at that, her shoulders went up once more. Shane wondered what she looked like without legs, with the sometimes tail.

"You figured it out," she said, though that wasn't totally true. She seemed to need to believe that, though, and so Shane nodded.

"I figured it out," he agreed, squeezing her hand, carefully, not quite sure how to hold onto it with the webbing.

Maya looked down at their hands, as if she'd just noticed they were joined. "They don't bother you?" she asked, after a moment.

He glanced at the scales, ran his thumb along the side of her palm where they were smaller, softer. "Why would they?" Truly, the scales were fascinating, a texture like a fish, but not, dry and smooth and slick without the moisture.

She lifted her other hand, spread it out. "It doesn't go away." She sounded a little dismayed, and he shifted up onto his knees to take her other hand.

"They're beautiful." He'd never seen anything like them, like her, truly, but what was wrong with that? What was wrong with liking something different, unique, wild, wonderful?

"I thought they'd be gone by now," she said, finally, letting her fingers settle along the line of his.

"Gone?" he repeated, surprised, turning her hand this

way and that, enchanted by the way the sun bounced off her skin.

A small sigh escaped her lips. "I've been on shore a long time," she told him, softly. "They say the longer you're on shore, the more the sea leaves you. But I still have those, the scales, there, where my tail once was…"

"Why would you want them gone?" he asked, perplexed; surely she was special, more special than most girls.

"They're ugly," she said, evenly. "On land, that isn't what you have."

"Then why don't you go back?" he asked, even as the words were more painful to utter than he could imagine. Her palm was cool against his, but he could feel her pulse beating where their skin touched, and, with each turn of her heart, of the blood in her veins, he could feel it in his own, and he felt dizzier every second.

"I can't." She sounded immeasurably sad, and he thought his own heart could have broken with her voice.

"You're trapped," he said, breathless. "You can't go back and you don't fit here."

She nodded, chest hitching, but no tears came to her eyes. "I thought — Trey said…" She pulled in a breath and he thought he could see the thin skin at her throat flare. "A life for a life."

"A life for a life," he echoed. Now, where the idea of her killing Trey or, at least, taking him to his foretold death, had horrified him, caused him to back away from her by the canals, he understood, and, indeed, his heart did break, and ache, and his eyes feel warm and wet.

"How did Trey know?" he asked, finally. He pushed his shoulders up, rubbed his ear against the point of one in a sort of tic, a habit that rose up from time to time when he was nervous, or sad.

She squinted against the sun. "I don't know," she said, but then shook her head, obviously dissatisfied with her own answer. "Trey knew things, you know? Just… without saying, without asking."

Shane found himself nodding: it had been something he could always file as coincidence, for the most part, like when he'd bring the kind of soda Shane liked or know when he'd be appearing in the doorway, his eyes trained on the front of the store. Trey was quiet, but always seemed to be watching, and knowing, and, now, it didn't seem like too much of a stretch to believe the guy knew about Maya, and knew how to make her scales disappear.

"Did he love you too?" he asked, and, this time, it didn't hurt quite as much to envision — Trey wasn't a bad person, and Shane could understand that sadness that always seemed to lurk in his eyes, unspoken.

"Lots of people love me," Maya said, and her voice echoed somehow, as though it were coming from somewhere far off, far away, long ago.

"But you didn't save Trey." He felt bad for pushing, especially when she bit her lip and her fingers went slack in his.

Shane tightened his grip on her hand. "You don't have to tell me," he told her quickly. "But, you know, if you do: I believe you. I'll always believe you."

She didn't smile, and her eyes were wide and colorless, or full of all the colors, he wasn't sure which. "You came with a different name. You said it, once, but then you told the police a different one. Why?"

He hadn't been expecting that, the change of direction, the focus turning to him, as hot and bright as a spotlight. It made him shift uncomfortably, and feel the sand creeping into the waistband of his jeans, over the cuffs of his socks.

"I ran away from home." It was a given, and, if she'd really been in Venice for long, she'd know that of course. All those teenagers, the ones that seemed to return, as it was, day after day, had floated up on shore just as surely as the seaweed, jellyfish, and gasping, dying fish.

"Why?" Her voice was simple, but achingly full, and he knew quite clearly that he couldn't prevent himself from answering.

"I wasn't wanted there anymore." He swallowed painfully, and looked away again, from her beautiful profile; gaze over the sand, it was much easier to breathe.

"I don't think that's true," she said, after a long moment in which they both breathed, just slightly out of sync, and mostly soundless against the nearby waves. "You don't seem like someone people would want to get rid of."

His laugh was hollow, meaner, than he meant it to be. "I think there are plenty of people who'd disagree with you," he said, glancing back at her. The expression on her face, sad, cut like a knife, and he looked away again quickly. "Louis for one."

Her fingers squeezed his again, even as his felt like they'd try to escape, dissolve like sand. "You really don't believe that, do you?"

"He doesn't seem to like me much. Now, at least," Shane added, lifting his other hand, grainy, to rub at his forehead. "'Specially with you here."

Her shoulder touched his, and he looked over, where she was hunched and worrying her lips in her teeth, but eyes still on him. "He's trying to protect you, Shane."

"From you?" he almost scoffed.

"Yes. From me." She swallowed, and looked down at her feet, her hands and their scales.

"I don't get it." He would have released her hand, but he liked it there, and, truly, if there was one thing he was afraid of, it was forcing her to leave.

"He loved me. Loves me," she corrected herself, nibbling at the soft skin of her lip with the flat of her teeth; they were small, white and straight. "He wouldn't have stayed here if he didn't. He's been watching me the whole time."

Shane shook his head. "He didn't know you. Just the girl on skates."

A smile appeared, fleeting as it was, and she went back to chewing. "Pretends. Because he knows what I am, who I am, what... happens when you love me."

"What?" She spoke in circles, and it was enchanting and irritating all at once.

"You die, of course," she said, mournfully. "Of course. Trey is dead, Donovan too. Did he ever tell you about Donovan?"

Trey had known of him, but not really Shane. He shook his head. She sighed.

"And Carson. And Jimmy."

"You killed them?" He hadn't meant to phrase it that way, but it was out before he could stop it; she flinched like she'd been shot.

"They died," she corrected him, softly. "And they loved me."

"Did you take them out like... like Trey?" His mind was reeling, and he felt nauseous-- seasick, ironically.

She shook her head. "Trey asked me to do that," she said, softly, but her voice was clear, precise, and he knew it was for his benefit. "Trey knew. Trey always knew, and he knew that it was the ocean that would take him. He just thought, you know, it would take me too. Help me. Finally free me."

"To be a human," Shane provided, though he wasn't sure he'd filled in the blanks right.

Maya tipped her head for a moment, and then shook it in disagreement. "That's not quite it," she said, thoughtfully. "I'm not. I can't be. Any more than you can change your skin color. It's more like... like a name." Again: that smile, moving like water over her face. "Make my name less dangerous to speak. Calmer waters."

He finally had to smile again, too. "Smooth sailing."

She shook her head just a little, but it was with something like a blush: her skin didn't quite allow for that, for the pinkening he might have seen on another girl, but he recognized it all the same.

"Thank you," she said, after another long moment, in which he'd not really noticed he'd been staring at her.

"Thank... me?" he asked, startled, and looked down at their joined hands, then back up at her face.

"Yeah," she said, easily, lifting her other hand to loop a long, tangled lock behind her ear, fingers lingering there before dragging along the line of her jaw to rest at the point of her chin. "For listening."

"Well, uh, of course?" That's what Shane was good at, had always been good at, but, moreover, he couldn't imagine not being willing to sit there, for hours, for days, listening to the sound of her voice.

"I say sad things," she said, almost apologetically. "People don't like sad things."

"I think," he said, reaching for her drifting hand, pulling it to his chin, and she raised her eyebrows, expression surprised and pleased. "You don't know much about my kind as you think you do."

And then she was smiling again, that dolphin laugh, and Shane could have done with the world ending, so long as it ended like that.

CHAPTER SEVENTEEN

There had never been a shade of ambition in Louis' surfing: he was out on the ocean because he had to be, not because he fancied any sort of higher calling. While good, exceptional, even, he had no designs on competitions, on making money. His board was low quality, and his van was always in disrepair, in a way that suggested not a sort of casual nonchalance but honest irresponsibility for vehicle ownership.

Louis wasn't made for much of anything else besides the water, and it was apparent to anyone who came across him. He spoke, but only just because it seemed required for him to get from point A to point B, those human interactions, brief as they were. He spoke, and he bathed, from time to time, but he did not cut his hair. He seemed incomplete without either his board and the waves, or, when land-bound, a cigarette in his hand, the smoke lifting a scent of tobacco that smelled not entirely unlike the spray of a skunk.

Louis came from money, as did more than a few of the sun-bleached and unruly young men who dotted the beaches in the seventies, unkempt and somewhat resembling the homeless men that shuffled along the paths at the top of the sand. The difference, of course, was not just youth, but some sort of carefree sense about them, the surfers, all only living for one thing: the next wave, the next slip and slide of the tide that would rise them up, ride them in, send them crashing down.

The money from whence he came was not his father's, but his father's father's: ranching, somewhere in the wilds of Montana, where Louis grew up. He lived a childhood of rolling hills and endless blue skies, and a yearning for the ocean that made yearly family trips-- to Hawaii, and to Florida-- something like a religious experience. The blue of the ocean was only a slight contrast to that of the sky over the horizon, and he swam as far as he could every moment he was loosed on the beach, and was rescued, more than once, by lifeguards, dragged away from destiny.

He was thirteen when he first got to try out a surfboard and, from that moment on, everything else was lost on him.

School days stretched long and pointless. He made only the most perfunctory efforts in class, turning in blank tests, or nothing at all, waiting for his eighteenth birthday, and trust fund, and the ocean.

He left on his while the candles on his cake were still smoking, hair curling long past his ears, a tin can of a car carrying him down the highway. He could have afforded something better, probably, but escape was more important, and he bought the first car that ran, and someone would sell him. He felt his heart race as he started the engine, every pulse and pump of his blood another foot, mile, laid down on his way to the water.

He didn't train, but was a natural. Louis found an apartment close to the beach and was at the shore every morning, waxing his board and humming to himself. There was a mystery about him that landed him girls, but he barely paid attention to them any longer than it took to hook up. Louis, truly, was not a heartbreaker, and it was made clear his skills were much more firmly rooted in surfing than in anything amorous.

Louis seemed charmed in most ways, but remained a

loner. It suited him, and he rarely noticed when he was being watched, or that more than a few others on the beach disliked him, hated him, even. Louis was easy to spot, even among the other tanned, blond guys out there, as serene as a monk in meditation, hair whipping in the salty air.

Every day seemed enchanted. That is, of course, until the day he met Maya.

***

Louis still woke in the night, gasping for air, as though under water, all these many years later. Going under was not a rare experience, naturally, and you learned to swim with the tide, to push for the surface, to keep your wits about you. It took an emptying of the head, a loss of thoughts, and maybe Louis never had much going on in his head, that sort of grateful stupidity, so that he popped up, like a cork, whenever he wiped out.

But nights he woke up gasping, flailing, and it took minutes, hours, sometimes, to bring his heart back down from racing. On those nights, he got up, lit a cigarette, and went to the window to watch the ocean.

He'd not gone in the water in more than twenty years, closer to thirty, and he didn't expect to go in unless he was damned well ready to die. She'd see to that.

Maya was an enigma, still. It pissed him off that she continued to have a hold on him, had a power that was inexplicable, was horrible and beautiful at once.

He knew Shane was with her; the boy never came back up the beach after he'd left him in the afternoon. He didn't think it meant he was dead: Louis did not have a second sense, or likely even a first, but he thought he knew when the boys died. He was sure he could smell it on the air, read it in the way the waves rolled in, and nothing had changed, but for a charge in his feet, through his veins, making him more irritable, restless, and achingly sad.

The record store saw less and less business, like a voodoo curse. It was an age of not just CDs, but digital music, something he could never understand, and refused to, both on principle and because his focus was utterly elsewhere. Louis didn't want to be a part of the now, and it showed. Louis always wore his intentions right on his face, and the scowl deepened, seemed etched into his skin, after Trey died, after Shane drifted away.

True: he'd been watching Maya for years. She was the reason he was still there, though his board moldered and rotted in the back of the storeroom, behind the boiler. He pretended not to participate, or pretended not to exist: an observer, a birdwatcher with a pair of high-powered binoculars, or, more accurately, a hunter with a gun. His sight was always trained on her as she spun by on her skates, his finger on the trigger but never really sure enough to pull it. He didn't know that he'd find that moment, that courage to take her out, before the ocean claimed him, too.

His eyes strayed in the direction of the rocks, as they always did when he woke late like this. It hadn't occurred to him until recently that she would return to the place he'd first seen her — with that many deaths hanging over her head, why return to the scene of the crime? That she skated down the boardwalk twice a day meant that she did not need to remain somewhat submerged in the water; that had been his original thought, why she never left the beach, why the furthest she seemed to move was to the canals.

He had figured her nature out early, the kind of creature she was. It wasn't as difficult to believe back then, maybe, or maybe he'd been sun-fried and wishful, and finding a mermaid out in the surf was a given, like a sailor after long nights at sea. He'd seen flashes of them before, he'd thought: silvery and quick-moving, like fish, with long hair trailing like snakes behind them. Others claimed to have seen them, too, and girls on the beach decorated their hair with sea shells, bronzed their skin and draped towels over their legs, flapping uselessly on shore.

But Maya had legs, and she wore a caftan in the wind, even as it stuck to her form with the weight of the water from which she emerged, outlining her lithe body in such a way that rendered it useless outside covering her scales. She had more then, too, covering her thighs down to her feet, her hands on up over her elbows and shoulders. She kept her hands tucked inside the long sleeves, but her smile had a watery quality that marked her as not quite a part of the scene on the beach: the surfers and smokers, the musicians and the performers who gathered even that many years ago, like a never-ending parade that had only just gotten started.

She was otherworldly, but not that pretty, not really. There were certainly beautiful women hanging out on the sand, with flat bellies and pert breasts, wide, white smiles and sun-bleached hair, hips that swayed when they walked. Maya was all rippling coolness, or still like the sky, staring openly and unapologetically, though she was rarely where she could be seen. She perched among her rocks with wide eyes, like a monk atop a mount, calm and outside, an observer only.

Maybe it was the flash of her silver scales, or a quick breath in through the gills that flexed and flared at the sides of her throat. Maybe Louis willed the image of a tail onto her long legs with an extra hit of acid, but he knew Maya was not of the walking world and, without a word, he fell in love with her.

It was easy enough, and, for a good long time, there was no complication in it, no need to discuss it, or so much as exchange even a greeting. He only knew a name by word of mouth, and he knew she watched him, the golden boy on the waves. Who wouldn't be drawn to the best on the beach? And so it was that day when the waves were killer and he'd ridden every last one in as though they were made of nothing more than a soft run of grass. When he landed close to where she perched, like a wet little bird, he threw down his board and scrambled atop the rocks. She was startled, colorless eyes wide, but she stayed locked in position, her caftan flapping around her, her tangled hair touching her feet the way she squatted.

"I'm Louis." It was not a graceful introduction but, once locked in her stare, he found nothing else to say but the truth.

"I know."

The storm moved in quickly, whistles travelling down the beach, towels rolled up, boards loaded. Everyone grumbled with annoyance, but they knew better than to go out in the storm, the lot of them, eyeing the waves that turned choppy and black as the clouds rolled towards them, having brewed far out from the shore.

Was it youthful stupidity that sent him out there? Pride? Was he a bit stoned? Perhaps all of it, but Louis charged out into the waves and he did not see Maya rise up on the rocks with her hand outstretched, and did not hear the horn that rose up to clear the beach.

He remembered little when he woke in the hospital with a shattered leg, a collapsed lung, stitches in his head. He remembered nothing but Maya's face before he turned away, the purse of her lips and the green tint that colored the thin skin around her eyes, the silver flash of teeth.

He was quite sure she meant to kill him, was the one who sent him in. She, the Oracle of the Sea, the harbinger of death and doom, the ancient symbol of danger, luring sailors to their end.

Louis was no sailor, and his travels were done. The money he had left in his trust fund from his father's father's money was sunk into a beachfront property, a storefront filled with dusty records and a business ledger that hadn't seen a major sale in fifteen years. It mattered little to him. His eyes, after all, were not on the till: they were on the ocean, the beach, watching her, her scales receding, her stance steadier and steadier on land.

Louis waited. He was more patient than she could have known.

CHAPTER EIGHTEEN

Shane did think about his mother. The dreams he had, the ones where he was not underwater, as he had been since he was a child, were of her. He didn't think the step-father would hurt her, but the nightmares worried that part of his brain: that the man had nothing to focus his rage upon, and used his fist on her face, that he broke and bruised her, and that Shane had left her to this, had given her a fate that she never deserved.

Those were the nightmares that made it so he tried to dodge sleep like a boxer, nightmares kept him awake even in the dim lights that fell over the alley or the side street. They were what kept him focusing his weary gaze on the few passerby, on the cars parked at the curb, the details of their hubcaps and handles, the lettering on the tires. The nightmares were rare, but painful enough that he had to avoid them at all costs.

Something about Maya, though, made it easy to sleep, and though they were there, on the beach, where the cops made their regular sweeps to scare away the street rabble, they were completely unmolested. Shane didn't know if there was something magical about Maya — of course there was, but more he didn't know if she had some power to keep them away, or make them invisible, or if there was some spell cast on the lot of the guys, so they let her do whatever she wanted.

It wasn't that far-fetched, really, in his mind: somehow Maya had existed for however many years and had never been run off, arrested, or even harmed. Maya was, of course, an enigma in every way: from her scales and tangled hair, to her quiet, ancient gaze, to her skates and ability to disappear and reappear at will.

They stayed there on the sand all day, and then he slept, and when he wrenched from sleep sometime in the dark, he was in her arms.

She was cold, in a way that was unshocking, but strange all the same: the few experiences he had sleeping that close to another person found him almost uncomfortably warm. His body remembered nights at the shelter with his mother, when they had no apartment to return to, the two of them squeezed into a narrow twin bed, her arms encircling him in a protective gesture, his back sweating and limbs stiff, but knowing better than to try to wiggle away. But Maya was different, and her arms were almost slack, as though simply covering him but offering no sort of restraint, or support, and he sat up slowly, in some attempt not to disturb her, but be free of her as well.

She woke anyway, her strange, glassy eyes blinking slowly up at him, her hair mingling with the sand. "Shane?" She didn't speak his name in the way that he did, the way it was presented to people, and he almost wanted to insist she call him Levron, knowing that would sound better on her lips and tongue.

"I'm okay." He knew that was why she worried, why her mouth was pulled into a pucker, and her fingers flexed as she stretched her arms. "Just a—a dream. No big."

"What kind of dream?" She sat up anyway, and pushed her feet in front of them, the paleness of her skin almost glowing in the faint light of the moon, her toes like pearls.

"Nothing really." But he was finding a certain inability to lie to her, and he shook his head almost immediately.

"I don't know. Not good, I guess," he confessed, lifting

a hand to rub at the back of his neck, itching and aching.

"About what?" Her voice was soft, and lulling, and he wanted to curl up in it like a kitten.

"My mom." He was almost surprised to hear the words in his voice himself: my mom. None of the street rats talked about parents, about a before. Unless it was a war story, something to prove your hardness, your capabilities, you spoke of nothing before your feet were on that particular bit of pavement. No one could live a totally blank life, of course, but there were no stories of a wonderful Christmas or a father who took you to the zoo. A reminder of the past, as small a token as it might be, was too much like a forgotten ember, never quite extinguished, and could only be trouble.

"I haven't seen her in a long time."

"Since you got here," she prompted; it was a given, of course, and she knew that, if he was talking about his mother that way, just in that tone of voice, there was no hate for her, and, if he had her, he would not be there, on that beach, in need of her. She laced her fingers with his.

"Yeah," he said, again, bobbing his head, eyes going to the black of the ocean, though it was hard to make out in that light. "She's not here. I mean, she's alive," he added, as that clearly needed to be said, had to be out in the air so he could assure himself it was still true. "But not here. I came a long way."

Shane turned their joined hands over, and pressed the back of his own into the wet sand.

"My step-father, he was an ass," he continued, rubbing his hoodie against his chin, the hair rasping over the fabric. "I don't know what she saw in him, but he was a drunk, and a jerk, and I couldn't stick around."

"Did he hurt you?" Her voice sounded like the water that flooded his ears in his other dreams, and though those dreams should have been more disturbing, maybe, than the ones of his mother, they were comforting, and so was she.

"Tried. Threw a punch. Last night I stayed there." He

still didn't know if that counted as cowardice, and he looked over at her, eyebrows furrowed, as though she could read his mind, knew the question, and could ferret out an answer for him.

"That's not okay," she said, squeezing his fingers with hers and leaning her shoulder to his. "Hurting other people, you know."

He breathed in, breathed out, and, of course, felt the guilt heavy in his chest, rising up his throat and feeling full and sticky.

"But I left my mom there," he said, and his voice sounded like the feeling of his throat, tangible.

Her hand was still around his and, for a moment, neither of them said anything, staring off into the darkness.

"I don't think she'd be mad at you," Maya said, finally, softly, barely over a whisper.

"Why would she?" she went on, turning in the sand so that she was facing his profile, his hand still in hers, resting in her lap as her legs folded under her, knees forming a bow.

"He—" Shane couldn't quite answer that, as he'd never really let the thought fully form, as it was.

"He what?" Maya had never pushed him, and she sounded unused to doing so, her voice trembling just a little, but she drew their joined hands closer, against her belly, under her breasts, and there she was warmer.

"He probably hit her," he said, squinting, though not sure why he was doing so.

"Probably," she agreed, to his surprise, and his head snapped around to look at her, teeth biting into his lip as his eyes blazed.

He was tempted to pull his hand from hers, but she was squeezing it with a strength she didn't look like she should or could possess.

"Probably he hit her," she said, and he could see her eyes shining in the dark, somehow. "But you didn't do that to her, did you?"

He faltered, and swallowed. "But I left her there."

"You didn't hit her. And if he hit her, maybe she left too."

It was a reasonable assumption, he supposed, and he'd certainly never thought of it. It brought him up short, and he turned to look out at the water he could hear more than see for a long minute.

"Do you think she'd look for me?" he asked, wearily.

"Maybe. Maybe she thought you could take care of yourself. Maybe she thought you were ready to go." Maya shrugged. "I don't know. I can't tell you."

Another long silence stretched out, and Shane shivered.

"Do you have a mom?" he asked, finally.

Maya shifted in the sand. This time, it was his turn to keep their hands solidly entwined.

"Yes, I do," she said, though her voice was strained and quiet. "Doesn't everyone?"

He shrugged. "It's not every day you get to ask a mermaid questions," he pointed out, a hint of a smile on his face, his gaze sliding to her though he didn't turn his head; he thought he saw a similar expression on her face.

"I have parents. And sisters." Her knees lifted off the sand and met, the bones kissing through her jeans.

"How many?" He did finally turn to look at her, genuine curiosity too strong not to.

"Ten." Her mouth lifted a little at one corner. "We're different."

"Ten," he repeated, breathing out with a shake of his head. "I don't have any. My dad left me and my mom before I was born. She said she never wanted any more 'cause I was enough."

She shrugged one shoulder. "There aren't many of us. So we're all kind of brothers and sisters anyway."

Naturally, then, he had to ask: "Don't you miss them?"

"Sometimes." She rested her chin on her knees for a moment before turning her cheek against the same spot, rubbing the soft flesh over and over the rise there, the fabric faintly rasping with the movement.

"It's been a long time," she continued, after such a long silence, he thought the subject might have been closed. He couldn't blame her for not talking — it was hard to talk about his mother and it had only been a couple years. She'd been there for decades without her family.

"They didn't like that I left," she said, licking at her lips. "We're allowed to leave, and everyone always came back. Until me."

"Really?" That sounded amazing, horrible and brave, and he wanted to kiss her again.

"I mean, there were others, a long time ago. My mother always said it got into one person, from time to time, and you never knew where it would crop up." She breathed out, and, again, he thought he could see the gills she mentioned, under her fluttering hair.

"It was like a disease, and warning, the temptation to stay on land. None of my sisters ever actually walked on land." She lifted her head and slid her heels along the sand until her legs were stretched out in front of her, toes pointed at the sky.

"Why did you?" he couldn't help but ask, both of them gazing down at the length of her limbs, long and skinny, sinew and denim, dusted in glittering sand.

"I wanted to know what it felt like," she said, tipping her feet towards each other, and then away, so that they looked like fins, for just a moment.

"Is it different?"

Maya nodded, and drew her legs up to her chest again. "Everything about it's different," she provided, as if that were enough to explain it all.

And, in a way, it was. Maybe he wasn't from the ocean, a different creature in different skin, but he was at the same time. Shane was hundreds of miles away from his family, his life, the boy he'd been before the night the step-father threw his fist towards his face. Being there, out there, he was like learning to breathe in a totally different way, to see through different eyes, and learning to move in with new arms and legs.

"I'm sorry," he said, though he wasn't really sorry at all.

She smiled slightly, her eyes crinkling at the corners. "Me too." And she didn't mean it either.

CHAPTER NINETEEN

It was the first time since he'd arrived in Venice that Shane didn't pass the phone booth, a relic from old times, but stopped instead. It was a narrow little room, and reeked of piss; surely no one used it anymore. He squinted against the ammonia smell just to peer in, before looking back over his shoulder at Maya.

They were inseparable, now, or, maybe, more like two halves of a previously united whole, brought back together. Shane was not a poetic person, but there was something deeply satisfying about having the girl by his side, a condition he'd not felt in years, and maybe in his entire life. Maybe he'd just been waiting for her all along.

"You don't have to do it," she reminded him, in that voice that never pushed or prodded, but seemed to somehow stay definitive anyhow.

"I know." And he did, but he was still standing at the broken folded doors, breathing in that pee smell that made the hairs in his nostrils tremble.

"You think the phone even works anymore?" he asked, after another moment, glancing in at the dull shine of the pay phone's side, the metallic cord looped and kinked, the receiver only barely in the cradle.

She looked into the booth over his shoulder, resting her chin there. He could feel her gills now, and she didn't move to hide them from him, same as her hands, though, on the street, she wore her gloves, and shoes covering her blue toes.

"I don't even know how they work," she remarked.

He smiled, and touched his cheek to hers. "Phone lines. And, um, connection boards. In the way old days, there were people who actually moved the calls by plugging them into the right spots, and you told them who you wanted to talk to when you picked up the phone."

"But now everyone has cell phones," she noted, hooking her fingers in the belt loops of his jeans.

Shane nodded. "Those use, um, satellites, I think. And cell towers. Radiation," he said, vaguely remembering worries about that, about growing tumors from holding cell phones so close to the brain. His mother had had a cheap one that opened like clam, and she only used it as a back-up; she didn't say it, but he knew she worried about that cancer.

He could feel Maya tremble just a little. "So is this safer?" she asked, sounding entirely unsure of herself.

"I have no idea," he admitted with a chuckle, turning his head enough to land a glancing kiss to the corner of her mouth, the smooth skin just beside it. "I guess so? I've never really thought about it."

They both went back to considering the phone, as though it were a particularly docile zoo animal, and might finally wake up and do something interesting. A red panda, or a slumbering monkey, the cage smoldering with the scent of its waste.

"You don't have to do this," she repeated, after many minutes ticked by, and people moved past them, the two of them occupying a certain section of the sidewalk that, though maybe a bit out of the way, was still there, on the main part of the strip.

"I know." He wasn't irritated, just perplexed, both by the phone, and the mere idea of calling his mother after all this time. It only fleetingly entered his head that he ran the risk of being tracked down, picked up, arrested, that his eighteenth birthday was still months off. He didn't know how any of that worked, though, if he would just be carted back home, or if they'd put him in prison or something. It made it so he was more afraid to hear her voice, years later, and maybe hear something other than happiness, something more like annoyance, disappointment, or disgust.

"We could get you a cell phone." Her voice was gentle, and Shane knew, now, when Maya was trying her hand at a joke.

"That would help," he agreed, before chuckling, and pushing them away from the phone booth so that he could wind his arm around her waist and steer her back down the boardwalk.

She wore her skates on the sidewalk. She told him she went dancing and walked the beach barefoot, but she didn't like to move up and down the street without her skates. It was something he couldn't really question, and it did make him wonder about the loss of her tail, of her ability to swim.

"If you called her," she asked, after a moment, as he steered her carefully down the sidewalk, a bit like a trolley, or a child's scooter; she never argued this, liking the feel of his hands on her hips, his head coming close to resting on her shoulder, their heights thrown into distinct disproportion by the wheels. "What would you say?"

Shane didn't answer immediately, listening to the thud of the wheels turning on the cement, knowing they were somewhat of a spectacle.

"I'd say hi," he decided, peering up at her, eyes squinting against the sun that always seemed to catch in the tangles of hair on her head, on the incandescence of her skin. "And tell her I miss her."

She tipped her head back and breathed in. "And then?"

"And that I'm sorry."

"Sorry for what?" It was a conversation they had in

119

circles, but one they, seemingly, never grew tired of. Each round picked another layer off, and they got closer to the truth, or, maybe, the actual call, still unmade.

"For running away."

"But you had to."

"I didn't."

She tipped up on her toes and caught herself on her stops. Shane ran into her backside, but she threw her arms out, balanced, and straightened up, goose-stepping so she could turn and face him.

"You were scared." Her eyes, that color that wasn't a color and was all of them at once, were the steely grey of the sky.

"That's not a reason." He stuck his hands back in his pockets, rolling back on his heels, her height even more exaggerated on her toes.

"Of course it is. If you weren't scared, why would you run?"

"Why wouldn't you?" They stared at each other for a long moment, and then he reached out and took her hand, sliding his fingers under her glove.

"What would you say if you could call?"

Her smile was crooked. "I'm sorry."

"For what?"

"For running away."

He kissed her fingers, she shook her head, and they turned to skate on.

Where Maya was the sole subject of an entire corner of the internet, something about having a companion made her both more visible and uninteresting at once. She had, of course, been oblivious to the eyes that watched her from all corners of the globe, and so this shift was nothing new. But Shane, who had been one of the sets of eyes watching her, ten and four, was surprised by the change.

He pushed her past Muscle Beach, past the drumming circle and the man eating fire, the silent guy with the monkey, the crazy old women who sold weavings out of a child's wagon. His hands on her hips, they were rendered invisible.

"Why did you skate?" he asked, to the back of her head.

It swiveled around, hair stirring like a living thing, over her tank top, the tangled tips around her waist, reaching for the pockets on the ass of her jeans.

"I told you," she said, eyebrows furrowed quizzically.

He shook his head. "I mean, ten and four, every day. Even in the rain."

"Oh." She looked ahead again, the navigator, before tipping her head back so that her chin thrust into the air, and she had to squint against the sun. "I never noticed the exact time. The tides, I guess."

He could hear tourists remarking on the heat, and he could feel it, too, the sun beating down on the back of his neck, the sweat forming under his arms and between his legs, the back of his knees, dribbling down to his socks. Summer was moving in on the beach, and though it was cooler the closer to the water, the sun was relentless, that famous California sunshine.

"I never would have thought of that," he admitted, looking down at her skates rolling over the uneven pavement.

Her chest vibrated a little with the rhythm of their travels, and a small laugh in her lungs.

"Your blood is nearly the same as the sea," she said, fingers finding his at her waist. "You never feel it? Restless? Like, for no reason?"

He was amazed at the cadences of her speech; for whatever reason, if he were to ponder the nature of a mermaid, he would have expected them to have an English accent, maybe, or not speak the language at all. Maya sounded like a girl, fifteen or sixteen years old, a Valley Girl bumming on the beach.

"I don't know," he said, after a minute's consideration.

"Maybe I'm restless all the time."

She tipped up on her stops again, but, this time, he was sort of expecting the halt.

"You should call her," she said, nodding decisively.

He wanted to kiss her. As it was, he wanted to kiss her all the time, wanted to be touching her, wanted to meld their skin together so he wouldn't be without her. It was irrational, and almost a little disgusting, frightening, but he didn't tell her, and wouldn't tell her. It seemed safer.

"I'm not sure I'm ready." There was more than that, but, at the bottom of it all: Shane was not ready. His mother's voice on the line seemed like the most dangerous thing in the world.

Maya nodded, fingers winding in his. "Is anyone really ever ready?"

He tipped up on his toes this time, and did kiss her. He could feel her smiling against his lips, the taste of her salty, like something sad, and something very far away.

CHAPTER TWENTY

In the end, though, he ushered Maya away when he finally went to make the call.

It was instinctive, in a way, this shutting off. He touched her lips with his fingers and her eyes were wide and understanding, her wheels already rolling her backwards down the sidewalk. She knew he was going to the payphone, the one with the graffiti that read strangely tender despite the close quarters, despite the rank smell.

Surely there were other payphones, or, indeed, cheap cell phones they could buy him. Maya had money, in some form, though he didn't quite understand how or where she got it, since her pockets were always empty and she had no real home, just a storage locker for her skates. There was something about going to the pay phone, that item that seemed like the most tangible link to his mother, hundreds of miles away, but with a phone that could ring and be lifted to her ear.

He stood against the nearby building first, though, staring up at the sun, the sky almost white with the brightness, the air like the inside of a furnace. Each blink turned lighter behind the lids, and he finally dropped his gaze to the cracks in the sidewalk, remembering the old story, likely from his mother, that he'd go blind if he stared at the sun. Still, spots exploded before his vision, even as he looked away, focused on the grey of the cement, the black of the tar filling old rends in the concrete.

He had two quarters in his hand, and a few more in his pocket. Shane had no idea how much a call to another state cost, really, but he figured a handful of change had to be enough. He didn't want to get anymore, at the very least; Shane didn't panhandle with any ability, and he and Maya had agreed to meet later, at the other end of the boardwalk, where she kept her skates.

Finally, he stepped inside the fetid little booth. The door was broken and would not close, but, as it was, he was not on a busy stretch, and, that time of the day, with the sun at its highest point, most people had been driven indoors, for a cool drink, or into the ocean for the same for their skin. He was dressed in his same jeans and t-shirt, sneakers, backpack, was practically alone there, and so no one could possibly overhear.

He dropped two quarters in the slot, and dialed the number that was still lodged in his brain, written in permanent marker on a wall in his skull, like the phone booth existed in his head as well. It was strange: throughout his childhood, he and his mother had had many numbers, many phones, too, connected and not, yet this number remained long after he had run to escape the apartment it was connected to. In a way, the others might have been more useful, like they might find him a way to reach back into time, and warn his much younger mother before she met the man who would fracture and scatter her family.

Holding the receiver was awkward, and it was only then that Shane realized he'd not made a single phone call in two years. It was a strange thing to notice, like noticing blinking or the sky. He'd not used the phone a lot back when he lived in the apartment: he just wasn't that kind of person, and his limited circle of friends all tended to live within shouting distance. That he'd not really done so much as touch a phone in months made the hunk of plastic and wire feel heavy in his hand, a foreign object, maybe living. Though he knew better, he tipped the mouthpiece near his chin and breathed in the metallic scent.

Over the speaker, the phone made a series of clicks and then, as if being projected through a tin tunnel, a trilling sounded. He could imagine, without trying, the sound of the phone his mother had in the corner of the apartment. Maybe it wasn't there anymore, maybe she'd bought a new one, maybe — and this was a thought that had not really entered his mind until that moment, even if, perhaps, it should have — she didn't even live there anymore. That he could be calling someone else then made his blood run cold, and he hung up before he knew it, fingers still clutching at the handle, sweat from his palm leaving a distinct print that remained for a moment after he lifted it away, only dissipated after another.

His hand hovered in the air for a long minute as he realized what he'd done. The quarters clicked down, dropping into the hold, lost despite the line not being answered; he'd not used a payphone in so long, he couldn't recall if this was standard procedure.

What if the number went nowhere? He knew the person on the other end of the line would be a stranger, with no idea of who the number had once belonged to or what had happened to her, and this made Shane step back out onto the street. He lifted his head again to stare up at the sun almost defiantly, a challenge, even as he felt tears gather, hot, behind his eyeballs. They pressed at the corners of his eyes, along the tender rim, and threaten to spill.

He was not good at self-pity, as it was, and Shane swallowed roughly, pushing the back of his hand and wrist over one eye, and the other, letting the bone at his joint dig into the softness there. Both of his eyes stung with the tears as he moved back into the phone booth.

He dropped his last coins in the slot and jabbed at the numbers with the tip of his finger, almost angrily, muttering each under his breath. The phone clicked, again, and then the tinny ring was in his ear again, and he gripped hard at the receiver, willing himself not to let go.

It clicked again, and then there was that weary voice, the one that was familiar and not. Shane was completely struck dumb for a long second, two, three, until she sighed into the receiver.

"Speak up or I'm hanging up." His mother had a low, melodic voice, one that could go threatening, but was mostly steady and strong. Right then, she sounded so tired, he almost didn't know where to stuff the emotions the sound brought up in his chest.

"Alright," she said, then, and he coughed, chasing the words before the receiver could leave her ear, and, with it, his last two quarters.

"Mama?"

He heard her breath catch on the other end of the line, and, in that held breath, the sound of the television behind her. She worked the night shift when he'd been there, and it sounded like maybe she still did.

"Levron?" There was no crack in her voice, no evidence of anything fragile; that was not who his mother was.

"S'me, Mama," he agreed, nodding as though she could see him, her agreeable little boy.

"Where are you?"

"I... that's not important." He couldn't say, and he hated himself for that, for the fear in her voice. "I'm okay."

"No, you're not. You're not here, not at home. Where are you?" She was not a person who could be redirected easily, and he remembered being completely unable to lie at her when his friends could do so, blithely, right to their parents' faces.

"Far away," he admitted, swallowing the desire to blurt California, or even the damned intersection of the phone booth in which he stood.

"Why?" There was just the slightest plaintive quality in the question, as short as it was. He brought his other hand up to grip at the phone, as though, by that gesture, he might be able to crawl in through the mouthpiece, through the miles and miles of wires, and into her arms.

"I had to go, Mama. I just... did."

She cleared her throat. "You never had to do such a thing." She dropped her voice, and he could hear the television again. "You're okay? No one's hurting you?"

"No, no. I'm fine, I'm fine." His voice raised, almost falsetto, desperate. "I'm okay, I'm good, I promise."

"Then you need to tell me where you are." She coughed, once, a forced-sounding clearing of the throat. "I'll trace the call, Levron. I'll call the police. You're on their files, missing person. They'll find you."

Part of him wanted her to do just that, but he knew better. He couldn't go back. Not until he was an adult himself, and not bound by a law to live with that asshole.

"I gotta go, Mama. I just — I just miss you. And wanted you to know I'm okay."

"I miss you, Levron. You don't even know." She sniffled, and his heart squeezed, hard, and his hands around the plastic, too.

"I'll come home someday. Promise. Just... not now."

"I'll call the police, Levron," she repeated, but he could hear the lack of conviction in her voice. Shane shook his head.

"I love you." But he had to hang up before she said it back, or he might have given up entirely, confessed his whereabouts, and ended up in the same room as the stepfather in a heartbeat.

Instead Shane — he was Shane there, not Levron, not in a long time — stepped out into the sunshine once more. Those few minutes in the dark, stinking darkness, made standing back on the sidewalk like entering another world, moving from one reality to the next. Every muscle in his body hurt, from his eyelids down to his toes, and he moved to sag against the nearby brick façade of a building, peering up at the white sky again.

He didn't know how long he stood there, but he was aware of the sound of Maya's wheels, now as familiar as his own heartbeat, over the concrete. He blinked, several times, but the brightness didn't clear, not right away, making her one more silvery spot in front of him.

"You talked to her?" Maya touched his face with her delicate fingertips, traced the line of his jaw and chin.

"Yeah." He couldn't straighten up just yet. He was effectively blind, though he wasn't worried, not quite — if he had just caused himself to go blind, he couldn't really see any fault in that. Sometimes things were meant to happen.

"She's okay?" Maya's voice was cool, but worried, and he licked his lips, like there was salt there.

"I think so. I don't know. I didn't ask." That sounded horrible to his ears, and he shook his head, even with it still in her hands, causing her thumbs to bump into his nose with the motion.

"What did you tell her?"

"Just, you know. I'm okay. I love her." He exhaled, blinked again; colors were starting to fill in, features and outlines, her eyes, all the colors, on his.

"I think she'll be okay," Maya said, in that soothing voice, like quiet rain. Her hands moved from his face to his shoulders, then down over his biceps and elbows, locating his fingers and lacing them with hers, as though weaving a basket between them.

"I know." Shane nodded and squeezed their hands together. Finally, he smiled, just a little.

"I think it'll leave her room to be mad at me when I can see her again."

Maya didn't have to ask his reasoning. Though her situation was quite unlike his, it wasn't at the same time:

once safety was insured, once his mother knew he was alive, she could be as pissed as she wanted at him.

"Just another couple months," she noted, pulling him away from the wall, rolling backwards on her skates.

"Just a couple more. Can you come with me?" he asked, then, blinking again; more details filling in with each flutter of his eyelids.

She shrugged. "I don't know." Her smile looked strange and glinting without his full eyesight.

"We'll see."

CHAPTER TWENTY-ONE

Maya knew she was pregnant almost the instant it happened. She wasn't really sure if this was a condition of her kind — that was not a conversation she'd ever had, nor had she been all that interested when she was young — or if she was just gifted in some way. The latter seemed possible, given what she had with Shane.

They'd kissed, and they'd laid in the sand, and he was the first who had seen the remaining scales, the ones that ran the length of her spine, over her thighs, the fin at the small of her back. He'd called her beautiful, and she believed it, and when she woke in the morning, before him, still in darkness, she knew she was pregnant.

She slipped away then, wading into the water up to her hips, and stood in the lapping waves to watch the sun rise. She'd left Shane with a smile on his sleeping face, the coal black of his lashes nearly lost against the deep brown of his face, cheeks almost the same color in the pre-dawn light. He was a delicate smudge against the white sand, and she turned her back on his sleeping form to squint out over the horizon. She listened to the water churn around her, higher and lower than the sounds of the cars on the nearby freeway.

He loved her, but that wasn't even a question. He loved her, but her kind did not need that. Water was a changeable element, always shifting, flowing, and love was the same: you attached, you drifted away. It was something she'd tried to understand all these years, and tried to show to boys she lead into the water and freed. Love was not static, it didn't stay.

Shane wanted to stay. His name was actually Levron and his mother, hundreds of miles away, loved him, missed him, and he owed her much more than he'd ever owed Maya, would owe her, no matter what he might think. A mother was different.

And perhaps that was why she felt that aching pull deep in her gut, now. She would be a mother, in several months' time, and maybe that was the love that didn't dissolve, only flowed outwards, expanding.

He was standing on the shore, at the waterline, when she turned to wade back up to the beach, her back to the orange and pink of the rapidly-rising sun. He looked worried, but it was a familiar expression, one she could smooth with her fingers and her mouth, and he helped her into her jeans, struck suddenly shy, biting his lips with a smile that seemed adhered to his mouth.

She felt guilty. She sent him up the beach, promised to come later. Maya did this, sometimes, but usually she stuck to her patch of rocks, breathing in the salt air, dragging her fingers along the watery culverts, lifting up shells formed in a place far away.

That morning, though, she waited for him to vanish wherever it was he'd go, and then she went up the beach, far up the beach, until she was level with the record shop. There she stood, staring up at it, knowing he'd be looking down.

Louis wanted her dead, Maya was aware. His was also a complicated sort of hate, sort of love, curious and sweet and painful. She waited for ten minutes before she made her way up the beach and arrived, barefoot, at his locked and barred door.

She was not expecting to find the store closed. Maya stood blinking in the now-bright morning, pulling at the ends of her locks, toes curling against the hardness of the concrete they rarely touched. If she knew she looked strange, looked like something dropped from another planet onto the boardwalk, it didn't show on her face. She stood, and she looked up and down the street, for no other reason than for something to do while she contemplated the situation. Because of this, she was not paying attention in the least when a hand came down over her mouth and an arm went around her waist and jerked her into the small alley that ran alongside the storefront.

His hand tasted of tobacco and pot, surf wax and cinnamon, and she choked only a little, going limp in an instant, the sheen of her skin slippery in that grip, her long body heavy. He grunted and managed to stagger into the backdoor of the record shop, dumping her on the floor of what she thought was a closet, and locked the door.

The small room was pitch black, and she lifted her hands to pat her confines, breathing rapid little pants through her mouth and nose, gills fluttering and flexing. She didn't panic, not yet, but she wasn't stupid, and her fingers found cleaning supplies, nose noting the rotting mold smell of an old mop, the chemical scent of cleansers and a pot of varnish, forever glued shut.

She found a shelf and lowered her rump onto it, tipping her chin up, her gaze going up into the inky blackness that was the same as the darkness at her feet. She could just make out her hand if she held it brushing her nose, a faint silver mass that had nothing with which to reflect.

There was movement outside the closet. She didn't speak, didn't cry for help. There was no doubt in her mind as to what had happened, and why, and why now, and so, all she could do was simply wait.

The smell of bleach was painful; her fingers curled on the seat she'd made for herself on the metal shelf. It was more efficient, easier, than bonds, than taking the time and risk to tie her up. The chemical vapor filled the air and kept her still, waiting for when he was ready for her.

It was hours later, by her judgment, and he looked wild and sad and unshaven when he opened the door. She raised one thin gloved hand in a wave. "You don't want to kill me."

Louis shook his head. "No tricks, Maya."

She nodded. "I don't have any."

He snorted, but he did let her out of the closet, which allowed her a breath not tainted by the chemical. Immediately, her head cleared, at least a little, and she took in the cluttered store room he'd released her into.

"You could have just let me in the front," she pointed out, though there was no snide tone in her voice.

He nodded in the direction of a broken-down chair and she sat, quite instinctively pulling her knees to her chest; it was her natural posture, but one with an added comfort, insulating what was to come.

Her eyes peered up at him through the gloom of a room that was boarded up, so that the only light filtered through the cracks by the window, and the cheap lamp on the table in the corner.

"I wanted you here on my terms." He sounded young, and tired, and she considered him from her perch, as he paced the short length of the room not cluttered with rotting boxes and furniture.

"What are your terms?" Her toes cupped the edge of the chair, and she rocked slightly, hands tucked around her ankles. She was confused, and she wasn't, but she wasn't scared, and she supposed that was a large part of his annoyance with her.

"You've got to leave him alone, Maya." His eyes were on hers and she stared up at him with her ageless gaze.

"I'm not going to hurt him." Her voice was small, but clear, calm.

Louis shook his head; his hair was wild and slipped out of the ponytail it was usually drawn into. He looked so much older than his years, a strange contrast to her.

"How many more do you plan to take?"

Not scared, but wounded, she drew her shoulders back. "I haven't done anything wrong."

"You prey on them, on us." He stood over her. Standing, she was roughly his height, but with her curled in the chair, he towered over her, and he seemed to fill the small room with his agony and desperation.

"Prey?" She blinked, slow, and tipped her head to the side.

"I can't let you leave here, Maya," he said, leaning in close. "I've let you do this long enough. No more."

"You need to let me go," she said, fingers tightening at her ankles, a tiny, creeping fear starting to tingle at the base of her spine.

"But if you go back out there, you'll give him up too. And I could have stopped you years ago."

She shook her head, pushed her way to her feet, hands up in front of her. In some combination of disgust and anger, he backed away so she couldn't touch him.

"You've been so scared of the ocean," she breathed. "Always. Even on your board. Why do you blame me?"

He snorted. "I was never afraid of the water until that day you threw me in."

"I didn't." Out of all of them, Maya had never so much as touched Louis: not on the beach all those years ago, and not now. "It was an accident, Louis. Things happen."

His back hit the table laden in old cassettes, sending a pile of them cascading to the floor with a frightful clatter. "I never wiped out like that before."

"Youth is fleeting, Louis."

"Not for you."

There was a faint smile on Maya's face, and she looked down at her form, at her dirty jeans and fitted shirt, the gloves on her hands.

"No, not for me." Not then, at least, though maybe whatever was inside her was truly the key, the one that would shed her body of her remaining scales, and her tether to the sea.

"You took Trey and Donovan, you took others."

She shook her head. "It was the same for them as for you," she said, softly. "I just was the companion."

"Your kind sinks ships. You still do."

She flinched, but only a little. "Maybe," she agreed. "And your kind destroys our home. Maybe it's tit for tat?"

"You think that?" He was shocked but, then, so was she, at her own words.

She considered it, the silence filling the air for a minute, two. "Not really." Why would she be there, otherwise? Why would she have given up her home, her family, that endless life, for concrete and noise and heat and harm?

"I should end you," Louis said, then. "All of it."

"Maybe," she agreed, tipped her chin to look at him through her eyelashes, silvery like water. "Do you want to?"

"Yes." But he made no move.

Her fingers found his chest, the first touch he'd ever had of hers, flattening against his tattered shirt. "It won't bring you freedom, not really."

"You don't know that," he breathed, but he was dizzy already. "Damn you…"

She smiled, just a little, and stepped away. The door to the alley was behind her, and she slid her gloved hand over the handle and turned it, the room filling with sunlight, inch by inch.

"I didn't mean to," she said, standing in the doorway, a silhouette surrounded by sunlight.

"What?" He had to ask, he couldn't make himself stop staring.

"Make you love me. I was just a girl on the rocks."

"You were never that," he countered, chest tight. "You never could be."

"Maybe." She tipped her head once more, stepping

back, receding into the alley. "Maybe not." And then he was left gasping as she slipped down the alley and out of sight.

CHAPTER TWENTY-TWO

The summer storms drowned out the beach every afternoon, and the girl on the skates vanished with them. It was unheard of, but something had changed about her in the past weeks, and when she disappeared in the mornings, too, was rarely spotted, out on the rocks, it seemed like a fundamental shift in the ways of the beach, the boardwalk.

And so, maybe, it wasn't a total shock when she was picked up by the police.

In reality, Maya wasn't surprised by it, either. Though she'd not seen Louis since the day she escaped from his storeroom, she was aware he was still watching, and waiting. Truly, she'd expected something more grandiose, and likely gross, violent, and extreme, than the cops.

She was alone; Shane had gone up to the souvenir shop that was happy to pass him a few bucks to hold a sign on the weekends. Maya stayed down near the water. It made her happy, standing there with her toes in the surf, the heat of the sun almost unbearable against her freckled shoulders. There was a need for such solitude, really, as much as she loved Shane: there was some sharing of a consciousness, now, with whatever was growing inside her, and knowledge of the loss of such a thing that she wasn't quite ready to let overtake just yet.

The police that came down the sand were fully

uniformed, and she felt bad for them, almost guilty. The cops that patrolled the boardwalk wore shorts and polos, rode bikes, but these were cops from the precinct, and they looked like foolish penguins trying to make their way down the sand in their slacks and shiny shoes, sweating under the brims of their caps. Their badges flashed in the sun and the gulls overhead made loud and interested noises as they sent a sort of Morse code into the air.

"Young lady," one panted once he was close to her; she'd made no move to get away, had known they were coming for her when the first commotion started. "We'd like you to come with us."

"For what?" she asked, standing, brushing the sand from her rear and thighs, the grains clinging to her gloves anyway.

"We have a few questions."

"Oh?" She regarded the two of them openly, looked up the beach at their similarly-dressed companion. They all looked away, gazes darting anywhere that was not her face.

"About some disappearances, miss," one provided, finally.

"Oh. Well, okay." Maybe they'd expected her to protest, or fight, but Maya had nothing to fight against, or fear. And maybe that's why they thought she certainly would bolt.

They lead her up the slope of beach back to the boardwalk, shaking sand from the upturned cuffs of their slacks. On the side-street was a car, and they put her in the back; it was only there that the smallest amount of fear crept into her narrow veins. The backseat was caged, and Maya's kind, as might have proved unsurprising, did not like being caged. She sat on her hands, though, breathed with her mouth, shoulders curled, and listened to the thud and hum of the engine as the cop behind the wheel started the car.

The wheels made a sticking noise as they rotated, the

warmed rubber pulling away from the gummy asphalt. The radio cracked and squawked, reports from other locations, the bustle of Los Angeles life and crime.

The ride was short, and she was ushered into the waxy-scented halls of the police department. It was the furthest she'd ever been from the ocean, and it made her skin feel tight and dry, her lips pained. Still, she followed along gamely, into a small, dank room with a table, a chair.

She was poured a glass of water. She wondered why everyone was being so careful.

"Miss—" the cop started, then stopped, clearly unsure of what to call her.

"Maya," she said, softly, voice a rasp, rocks tumbling into the sea.

"Maya. Do you have a last name, Maya?"

She shook her head. Truly, it wasn't all that uncommon, the freaks the police picked up down on Venice Beach, many of them going by only one name, or a fake name, something supposedly spiritual, or nothing at all. Maya knew there was at least one performer who went by a symbol.

"Maya, we have a few questions for you about some missing people." She knew that was what she was there for, and listed them in her head, though her eyes stayed on the policeman's placid face; he was not one of the ones from the beach.

"Trey Lazen, and Donovan Perry-Murdock. Do these names ring any bells?"

She tipped her head to the side. "I've never heard them like that. Perry-Murdock, that's a nice name." She enjoyed the sounds of the spoken words, so smooth and suddenly hard.

The cop eyed her. "So do you know them?"

"Oh. Yes, I do. Trey and Donovan."

"They're both missing. Listed missing, by, uh, interested parties." No use beating around the bush with that one: like most people down on the boardwalk, they hardly had a family to report them missing.

"I know," she said, and there was a sorrowful tone to her voice; Maya shook her head. "They were nice."

"We were told you might know where they are."

She shook her head no, and then nodded yes, then shook it again.

The policeman looked annoyed. "Can you give me a clear answer, miss? Out loud."

Maya shook her head once more. "I can't really tell you where they are. No one can, I think."

"Why is that?"

"Because no one can really say where they went. Only they know that."

He sighed, and leaned his arms against the table. "Where do you think they went?"

"Back to the universe," she said, simply, her gaze open and simple and hundreds of miles wide and long.

"Pardon?"

She shrugged. "They were given back to where they came from."

He looked down at the file on the surface in front of him. "Mr. Lazen is from Topeka. Perry-Murdock from Texas. You mean they went back home?"

Another shake of the head, and a nod in turn from Maya. "Not there, but there, yes, home."

He shuffled the papers in the folders, and she sat quietly, wondering when they'd let her go. Maya wasn't stupid, even if she never quite understood the interactions and motivations of the legged people. She knew there was some belief, in the man's heart, in the files before him, that she'd done something wrong.

She wasn't stupid, and did not have to rack her brain. In fact, the defense was on the tip of her tongue, though she knew better than to declare it. She had taken Trey, and Donovan, out there in the ocean, in that effort to set them all free. But she had not forced them, and that was as true in her mind as it had been when they each took her hand. Donovan, she'd argued with, had tried to run from; she opened his jeans and begged with her mouth, but he asked and asked and asked, and she took him out and watched him disappear. She'd drug her feet with Trey, whimpered and whined, and still the same thing.

The ocean was to blame, if anything, and she knew there was no blame in the wax and wane of the moon.

"Maya," the cop said, finally, with a steely hard gaze. "Do you know what happened to these young men?"

She shrugged, and looked towards the door, the small bit of glass set inside it near the top, crisscrossed with chicken wire to make it impossible to break. She knew these things, without knowing, and knew that she wouldn't try to escape at the same time they'd never find a way to hold her.

"Maya, I'm going to need a yes or no answer."

Maya had never lied, not to her knowledge. She was not capable of lying, not with her tail, not with scales that coated her eyelids and kept her from crying too.

But she shook her head. "No, I don't. I don't know what happened."

It was like the ringing of a bell, the shattering of glass that was not reinforced by wires. Her shoulders ached all of a sudden, and her stomach, and, for one long moment, she pressed her hand over the very small swell of her belly and held her breath.

The police officer stacked and restacked the files, righting their angles with his thumb, pressing the meat of the digit over each name.

"Alright," he said, finally, tapping them on the table, laying them down, lifting them again and tapping them once more. "You're free to go."

She stared, unblinking, and then nodded, getting to her feet unsteadily. She was barefoot, as usual, and the tile was cold against her soles, colder than she remembered it being as she was walked down the hall. The whole room was cold, vile and drafty, and she crossed her arms to cup her elbows in each hand, waiting for him to unlock the big door and set her free into the hall.

They didn't offer her a ride. She was miles from the beach. She sat at the bus stop, bowed her head and wept.

CHAPTER TWENTY-THREE

Shane wove his way down the boardwalk in the direction of the rocks. In his hand, he clutched a bag of the pastries the woman with the cart had pressed on him for free earlier that day, and he'd kept at his feet out on the sidewalk. They were sticky from the heat, and the bag was spotted with grease, but he could smell the sugar even with it hanging at his side, and it made his stomach churn slightly with a sort of primal desire brought about by not eating for days at a time.

He'd made thirty dollars that day, far more than usual, but the owner of the shop felt guilty for having Shane stand in the sun for so long, and slipped him an extra ten from the till. He'd shoved the bills down into his sneaker, the best place for them while he was walking, though he would transfer them to his pocket later—incidentally a safer spot for a kid on the street. The things he'd learned in the past several years.

The beach and boardwalk were in a lull at that time in the afternoon: late, hot, and most people had retreated to the shade and into the stores and restaurants for air conditioning and cold drinks until the weather mellowed. Shane liked it when the beach was quiet, and bright; despite having stood out in the light and heat all day, there was something restful about feeling too warm, feeling baked down to the bones, loose and relaxed. He'd tied his hoodie sleeves around his waist, and the fabric flapped against his legs as he walked, sweat trickling down the back of his neck with the speed of snails on pavement, sticky and slow.

He shifted the bag from one hand to the other as he stepped out into the sand, the weight of his body making him sink slightly, that always surprising disequilibrium that made his head reel for just a moment. He looked out over the shining water of the ocean, bright blue and endless, disappearing into a haze at the horizon, and he breathed in deeply, tasting salt on his lips.

The water was always louder down at the edge of the rocks, no matter the time or the tide. It was like static on a television set to Shane now, a pleasant sort of annoyance, made tolerable by the appearance of Maya as he climbed up over the rocks to the spot she loved best, the hollow where she could sit with her knees drawn up and gloves off, and be sprayed by the water.

That afternoon, though, she was not there, and he held the rocks precariously with both hands, the bag caught in the fingers of his left. It didn't occur to him, not immediately, at least, to be surprised by this: sometimes she vanished, and then she would reappear, as randomly and suddenly as a mirage, herself, glittering in the sunlight, made up of almost insubstantial stuff. Those days he'd have to kiss her, hard, to confirm that she was there at all.

That day she was not, and it brought Shane up short, enough that he didn't notice one of the more jagged rocks digging into his bare palm until blood welled and made him slip slightly.

He climbed back down to set the bag of pastries on the sand and considered his palm. It wasn't a deep cut, but enough that the blood was bright red and slick, and he didn't relish the idea of smearing the stuff on his jeans. Finally, he shook off what he could, picked the bag back up, and walked up the beach.

He didn't have a destination in mind, but one minded him, and he was looking down at the cut again when a shadow fell over him and he glanced up to find Louis. The man was backlit, and so it was just his stance — slightly sloped to the side to accommodate his bum leg — and the outline of his wild hair that indicated who was standing before Shane.

He stopped, and then stepped back, still holding his palm up so that the blood, while he stood in such a way, rolled back down over his wrist, under the woven bracelet there.

"What happened?" the man asked, inclining his chin.

Shane couldn't see his face, and so couldn't see his expression, and he took a gamble. "Just cut it. Nothing big." He cupped his hand, fingers curling in; the pain increased sort of out of nowhere, but he just shook his head against it.

"You should clean it out. All kinds of shit out there that can cause a nasty infection. Come on." Louis was already heading into the record shop, which Shane swore he'd not seen open in weeks, though, admittedly, he'd not walked up that direction from the beach in the same amount of time. It was the look of the store that told him it was shuttered and still and, even up close, now, it looked the same, strange and silent and sad, somewhat like a tomb. Shane felt weird about going in, hesitant, and he stood there, greasy bag in one hand and cupped bleeding one held up before him like an injured paw as Louis unlocked the door.

The air that flooded out was cold and musty, and Shane wrinkled his nose. There was something forbidding about the dark shop, and he found his feet suddenly leaden, and certainly didn't want to go inside though he couldn't quite understand why that was so.

"Kid," Louis sighed; he was grey, Shane could see, now, in the shade, from head to toe, though his shirt was the same blue plaid as usual, though his skin was sun-crisped and his eyes were still a sharp blue. Still, everything about him was grey, as though the color had been sucked away, or a television had its colors turned down, and Shane stared at him openly for a long moment before he allowed himself to step inside the store.

It felt as though he had been swallowed by something living and, for one long, suspended moment, Shane inwardly panicked. He knew he had gotten flippant in recent weeks, easy, there with Maya by his side, with her strange, shimmery magic, and it was stupid to have followed Louis into the store, wound or no wound.

The store reeked of chlorine, like some kind of chemical burp from deep in the bowels and, looking up, Shane could see it had not been used to clean in any manner. If anything, the store was dirtier than he remembered it, everything coated in a layer of dust so thick, it appeared like fur. That was why it was stifling, he thought, why it felt like he was being smothered, slowly pushed down the gullet of a monster that he couldn't begin to comprehend.

He snapped to, and Louis was already disappearing into the back room where the ancient first aid kit resided. Shane cupped his hand again and looked down at the blood pooling between the lines of his palm, black in the dim light of the store. It wasn't enough to make him dizzy, but the overwhelming scent of bleach was.

"Comere." Louis' voice was sounding from the back, and it was deeper than Shane recalled. In fact, everything in the store had taken on a quality he didn't recall, and he moved very slowly through the stacks of records, both out of a sort of fear, and because it felt like his feet weighed a thousand pounds quite out of nowhere.

He found the older man at his crowded desk with the kit, and the smell of bleach was even heavier there. The floor, too, was sticky, and Shane looked down at it, lifting his sneakers off the tile and feeling the rubber having to break away from the mottled surface.

Louis did not comment, but had a bottle of peroxide in his hand. Shane cringed as he seized his hand, poured the liquid over it; it sizzled and popped. With a towel that was grey in the gloom, hardly the bastion of cleanliness, he wiped away the bloody mixture, and then set about wrapping a bandage around Shane's hand. It was old fashioned, like he was dressing a war wound, and Shane stared at Louis working, dumb.

"You cut it on the rocks," Louis guessing, breaking the long silence, and Shane had to nod. Louis grimaced.

"She's not coming back," he said, tying off the long strip of bandage, and Shane snatched his hand back just as he did, his brain suddenly clearing from the chemical fog.

"What are you talking about?" He forced himself to meet the old man's gaze, as much as he didn't want to.

"The cops picked her up this morning. For killing those boys. All of them." He sounded matter-of-fact, almost weary, and so, though Shane's uninjured hand curled into a fist, he could not swing out and strike Louis in the face.

"What did you do?" He could barely speak; the words seemed trapped somewhere between his chest and his mouth, caught in his throat like a fish bone, painful and unyielding, spines digging in.

"She got what was coming from this side," Louis said, simply, looking down at Shane's hand, at the bit of blood that was not wiped away at his wrist, a slash of black against dark skin.

"You called the cops on her?" Shane took a stab at it, an easy one: how else would Maya have been picked up, accused, arrested? No one else on the beach, the boardwalk, knew who she was, what she was, anything about her — just knew her long hair, her skates, her smile. Maya was a mystery, the Venice enigma among the freaks and weirdoes, and none of them would call on her, would break her.

Louis, though, shook his head. "She had to know it would catch up with her."

"You're a fucking liar. You know that Maya hasn't done anything. To anyone." Shane could feel a fury rising in him, unfamiliar, hot and choking. His eyes blazed in the half-light of the room, his heart slamming in his chest.

"She killed them!" Louis was facing him, fully now, and his hands came down hard on the desk, hard enough to displace a stack of albums, sending them cascading to the floor with a strange grinding sound. "It's finally time she's been stopped."

Shane breathed in, caught another whiff of the bleach, and gagged a little, his throat still full of something sticky and complicated.

"You tried," he realized, blinking. The scent seemed somehow stronger all of a sudden, even as Louis had not moved, and Shane hadn't even seen a bottle. "You were going to do it."

Louis snorted. "Big words there, boy."

"Don't call me boy," Shane said, through gritted teeth, his jaw clenched so hard, he could feel is pulse against his temples, beating like a drum, the scent of blood mingling with that of bleach, a terrible combination.

"You're a child," Louis told him, his voice gone steady again, young in a way that Shane had never heard it. His eyes, too, were from some time else, from a time long before Levron had even shown up on the beach, from a time, maybe, when even Maya was still a child, too.

"There is danger in things that look pretty."

Shane breathed out, forced himself to loosen his jaw, his shoulders, lest the tension cripple him. He knew how to run, but also knew the reach of Louis' grasp, and that he'd never make it through this dark maze of a store before the old man, hobbled, snatched him back.

Would he? Shane stared at him, openly. The room stank of the bleach while everything else in the store was dusty, dirty, cold and unmoved. Maya had to have been there. Louis had to have tried before giving in to the authorities he otherwise hated.

"Why do you hate her?" Shane asked, finally, shivering under the other man's gaze.

Louis didn't answer, not at first. He packed away the first aid kit, apparently satisfied that Shane wouldn't bolt, and clicked each buckle on the metal box shut.

"She destroys everything she touches," he said, finally, and, again, he sounded old, sad and weary.

"She didn't destroy you," Shane attempted, but, of course, he knew so little, and Louis shook his head.

"She will, someday. She just hasn't managed to yet."

Shane waited, but Louis didn't continue. He edged towards the doorway, injured hand held close to his belly. The old man didn't move, but he did watch after him.

"She'll destroy you, too, kid," he said, a sigh escaping his lips.

"She won't," Shane argued, though his voice had dropped, almost soft, the fish bone dislodged. "She saved you."

Another shake of the head from Louis. "You know nothing, still, do you?"

But Shane was already moving, and, a moment later, the bell over the door trilled and he was gone.

CHAPTER TWENTY-FOUR

It took him an hour to find the police station, and then a good ten minutes to make himself go in. Shane knew he was running a massive risk going into the police station: he was a runaway, reported, a known panhandler, a street rat, a risk, a threat, all of those things. He'd seen what had happened to other kids who had gone to cops in a perfectly innocent quest, to either bail out a friend or report an actual crime, and end up dropped into foster care, the bogeyman of the street kids. Shane was inching closer to his eighteenth birthday, but there was time to capture him, and time to send him back over the hundreds of miles, away from the ocean and away from Maya.

That Maya was in the police station, that Maya was the one person he gave a damn about just then, made the decision for him. His focus narrowed and went laser thin on her. After all, if he feared losing her by going in, he'd never even chance to get her back.

She wasn't there. She had been released nearly two hours before, and that made Shane's head whirl. How had they not seen each other, how was she not back at the beach? Maya had told him she didn't need the water, not in a sort of life-sustaining way, but she did need it in an emotional way, a purely selfish way, even, and she wouldn't take a trip around town, over the burning concrete of the city. She couldn't possibly have her skates.

Where had she gone?

Whatever fear he had of the cops vanished, and they let him go. Shane wouldn't have known if they'd fingerprinted him and taken photos, he was so deep inside his head, scrambling for an idea of where Maya had gone. What if Louis had sent someone after her? What if he'd caught Shane to make sure there was time?

Out on the sidewalk again, he shook his head. That was a ridiculous thought: Louis thought her dangerous, but he was hardly the type of person to send a hit man after a skinny girl, no matter what kind of magic she held. He'd tried to capture and kill her himself, as it was: the bleach smell permeating the storeroom spoke to that.

He sat down on the curb. Could he really trust that, though? Louis had no friends, and spent his time smoking cigarettes or weed, staring at the water. He barely did business. It was only now that Shane was starting to piece together why that was so. It meant he had very little idea what the old man was capable of.

Shane rubbed his hand over his face and moaned without hearing it. It was hot in the city, and there was no promise of a cool breeze from the ocean like on the boardwalk. He hated LA: the buildings and the cars, the smog and rushing people. Even his kind, the street rats, they were different away from the beach, somehow more frightening, ragged and hopeless. The whole place filled him with dread, and caused his stomach to knot.

He stood and looked up and down the block in front of the police station. Where would Maya go? He tried to pose it like a simple scavenger hunt, if just to keep him from choking on his own breaths. The fact that she had not gone back to the beach, back to her rocks, was something he had to force out of his mind. She had gone somewhere else. He just had to find it.

He found Maya a mere block away. It was both sheer coincidence — he'd almost gone the other direction, after all — and the fact that she had not moved since she'd been released from questioning. The bus stop had been an easy destination when she turned left on the sidewalk: a bench on which to sit, that was all. She was still staring at her bare feet, blackened on the bottom, and aching, gravel clinging to the fleshy part of her arches. She didn't even notice Shane approach, despite him suddenly breaking into a run at the sight of her, the sloppiness of his footfalls.

"There you are!" He sounded just like his mother, but that, too, had to be pushed from his mind. He nearly tripped in front of her, but managed to squat instead, hands going to her thighs, and hips, squeezing there.

She blinked. For a long moment, she couldn't believe he'd appeared: Shane with his big, sad, dark eyes and the worried furrow of his brow, the sweat on his forehead scented the same as the ocean. She raised one hand, and then the other, to cup his face, thumbs pressing over the rounded parts of his cheeks, and then she was crying again.

"Hey, you're okay." The panic was still there, but replaced by the absolute, overwhelming gratitude that he'd found her. He put his hands to her waist, then, and wiggled closer, so they were clutched in some kind of hug, though she was almost clenching at his face, shoulders shuddering with her tears.

"I'm not," she protested. Maya was striking at normal times, and strangely beautiful then, with her tangled hair and sunburned face, her tears sparkling like sun off the waves. She was too far from home, he knew that, but, all the same, she looked just like the creature she was: something otherworldly, and extraordinary.

"You're okay. I'll make you okay," he amended immediately, pulling her closer, trying to close that last gap of space between them, meld them together so that she couldn't be taken away again. "You just come with me, okay, Maya? Come with me and we'll be okay, we'll get back home."

She shook her head. "It doesn't matter. They're going

to come back. They don't believe me."

"Who? What?" They'd taken her in, just for questioning, but that couldn't be good.

He scraped her hair from her wet cheeks before she could gather herself enough to answer. "They can't come back for you. I won't let them. We can leave."

It was out in the air even before, really, he'd thought it all the way out, but he knew it was true immediately, at least for him. They could leave. There was no reason to stay, not one. They could find another beach, another part of the ocean, and be safe there. Mexico, maybe — it couldn't be that hard to slip past the border, not with Maya. The water would be even warmer there, and the cops wouldn't be able to find them, wouldn't be able to take either of them away.

Again, Maya shook her head. "That's not how it works." Her voice sounded old, ancient, and pained, and she finally slipped her hands from his face to the back of his neck, stroking the tendons there before her fingers laced together to keep a strong hold on him.

"How does it work, then? Why can't we leave?" His gaze was searching her face, all swollen and tear-streaked, her eyes red and wide, eyelashes stuck together unnaturally.

"I have to stay."

"Why?" The way she spoke, sometimes, was almost enraging: Maya couldn't really answer in a straight way and, while that was hypnotizing sometimes, beautiful, it was also difficult to navigate when he was scared.

"That's home." He'd called it that, and there was no folly in such a title. The ocean was where she was from, but that spot, Venice, was where she'd put down her feet, and that was her home.

"Home is wherever you want it to be," he argued, frowning now, feeling that tightness coming back to his chest. "Home doesn't have to stay in one place. Home can be anywhere."

She shook her head again, hair stirring in an almost watery sound. "Not for me."

Shane understood, and he didn't: how could he? He'd run from one end of the country to the other, had sought out the sea without much conscious thought. He could see himself moving away, down to Mexico, up to Canada where you could watch the whales from the rocks, or, if they could, inland, to the Great Lakes, or even to the Great Salt Lake, the strangeness of which he'd always been curious, on the vast plains of Utah. There were billions of places in the world he could imagine his feet treading, and she couldn't move past her tiny outcropping of rocks.

He breathed out, petting the arch of her ribs with his thumbs unconsciously. "Then what do we do?"

She shook her head. "Let's go home. Please?" Her voice was plaintive, and eyes wide and sad and still brimming with tears. He wanted to kiss each one closed, taste the salt on his lips, and hide them both in her cave for the rest of eternity.

That, he understood.

And so he helped her to her feet and wrapped his arm around her waist. She leaned against him with a sigh, and moved almost painfully, slowly, down the block. The walk was not too long, but it was drudgery, out there in the oven-blast heat of the LA air.

CHAPTER TWENTY-FIVE

They hid.

It was easy and it wasn't, there in the freak show that was Venice Beach. Shane was any other homeless kid in dirty jeans and a stocking cap, and Maya had been weaving in and out of visibility for years, had been existing for so long on the beach that she simultaneously was a fixture and was completely forgettable.

They stayed by the rocks, and Maya stood in her wet jeans and tank top, her woven fingerless gloves, between them, skin shimmering with constant spray. Shane was not as hardy, and caught cold too soon, and so he climbed, favoring his injured hand, up the rocks and over them into the sunshine.

They didn't talk much — there was nothing that could be said. They kissed, and found one another's bodies under the clothes, but they didn't talk. Shane didn't know what to ask her, and Maya didn't have the words to answer.

The days stretched longer as summer approached, and Maya's belly slowly started to swell. She'd had no reason to take a pregnancy test, nor did they even think of needing a doctor: they didn't exist in the world of everyone else.

Shane only ventured up to the boardwalk to snag enough money for food to keep his rumbling stomach quiet. He rarely saw Maya eat - another mystery about her.

Her diet seemed to be made of the sun and the water, magically self-sustaining, like a plant that fed off air.

More people, performers and street rats and grifters, gravitated towards the bustling beach, and it got harder to hustle for money. Shane skipped eating some days, and the sun hurt his eyes. It was June, then, when he called his mother again.

It was both an act of desperation and one stupidity, one of bone-deep weariness. The phone was snatched up immediately, the call accepted, and, instantly, her voice filled his ear.

"Please don't hang up, baby, please don't hang up."

He hung up.

Shane wove down the boardwalk with his head tucked low, his chin brushing the worn fabric of his shirt. His birthday was approaching, but they were still in some limbo, where an unknown darkness could spring up at any moment, yet, when it did, Shane was still surprised.

He trudged down the sand, watching his shoes sink and the grains cover the toes. It was hypnotizing, and he was nearly to the water before he looked up, turned to face the rocks.

Police.

Running through sand, he'd heard once, was considered a great workout, and he understood that now. His brain latched onto that thought as he struggled against the resistance of the constantly-shifting ground, sweat rolling down his forehead and stinging his eyes.

His clothes were soaked and he was choking on the breaths he couldn't pull in once he reached the rocks. The police already had Maya, and she was handcuffed, her tangled hair limp around her shoulders. She was visibly pregnant, to anyone, now, and her shirt stretched tight over her belly; where it rode up over her hips, he could see the shimmering scales she kept covered.

Shane pushed his way forward. "What's happening?"

he all but yelled, eyes wide and wild, still stinging, with sweat and something else.

"Please back away, son," one of the officers said, stretching his arm, hand spread, to block the way.

Shane ducked, instinct, and pushed his way forward. Maya was sitting on one of the rocks, and her feet were, as always, bare, and pushed hard into the sand. She looked up at the sound of his voice and shook her head.

"Maya, I'm not going to leave you like this," he said, with heaving breaths, nearly tripping when another officer caught him by the elbow and yanked him back.

"She didn't do anything!" he yelled, and did fall, with a hard thump, colors dancing before his eyes with the jarring sensation. The officer had lost his grip, but stood over him, a black silhouette against the sun.

"Please don't get yourself in trouble, boy."

Rage swelled up in Shane and he fought his way to his feet, against the police keeping him there; below, against the uncertainty of the sand under him, against the fatigue and starvation that was slowly eating away at his insides.

"Maya, I'll come find you." His voice was steadier than he'd ever heard it, and her chin lifted, eyes flashing. She was warning him, but he shook his head. He couldn't let her go to jail.

He broke into a run, again, and they let him. He was faster, now, running on his toes, and, at the payphone, he punched in the numbers almost too hard, fingertips slipping over the worn metal.

His mother picked up again, already begging. He cut her off.

"Mama, I need your help, right away."

"Come home, I can help you, just come home."

"I am home."

There was a long silence on the line. And then: "I miss you so much, Levron."

Shane breathed out. "I know. But... Please help?"

His mother had never had much money, but she agreed

to wire him what there was, to the Western Union down the block. He had no idea if there would be a bail for Maya, how much it would cost, but he had fifty dollars in his shoe, and whatever his mother was sending, and that had to do something, he thought. It had to be at least enough to hire someone, to get someone to listen.

He had the money in his hand in an hour. The police had taken Maya away, and another unit was combing the beach. The street kids watched Shane with steely gazes from under the shade of the palm trees just off the boardwalk. Shane was never one of them, and they knew, somehow, that he was responsible for the sudden overwhelm of police.

He ignored them; there had to be something about his expression that kept them at bay, the set of his shoulders, his step.

The record shop looked shuttered, as usual, but he yanked the door open, charged inside. Louis was seated at the counter, as if expecting him, and Shane smacked both hands down on the surface.

"Give me everything in the register."

Louis lit a cigarette; it seemed to take forever, from taking the pack out, selecting one, lifting it to his mouth, grasping the lighter, striking the flint. Shane was breathing heavily, and wanted to knock the old man down, off his stool, pummel him, maybe, but he stood, palms burning, glaring across at him.

"You're not going to get her out."

"Fuck you."

Louis chuckled, but he sounded sad. Shane tried not to notice, but it was etched in the deep lines around the man's light-colored eyes, in the twist of his mouth.

"You can still save yourself."

"Give me the money. Now."

Louis shrugged, popped open the drawer with the old-fashioned ring that made Shane's teeth stand on edge, his tongue suddenly coated in the taste of something metallic, like a mouthful of pennies. There wasn't much there, there never was, but Louis withdrew twenties and tens, mostly a pile of ones, and counted them carefully.

In the end, between the money in his shoe, the money wired from his mother, the money from Louis, Shane had three thousand dollars. He folded the bills over themselves and stuffed the bundle into the waistband of his boxers.

"You'll still pay for this," he informed Louis; for once, his tone was as angry, as threatening, as he felt.

The man exhaled a cloud of smoke that seemed to have a face. "I know."

Shane slammed through the door and back out onto the street, the bright sun, the scorching air.

It took only another half hour, against traffic, for Shane to arrive at the police station. Unlike his last visit there, there was no hesitation: he pounded up the steps of the precinct and right through the old doors, squeaking on their hinges. The inside of the building was nearly as hot as it was outside, but stuffy, the air thick and heavy, and almost weighted down around his shoulders. He pushed his way to the counter, through people milling about waiting for their own arrested friends and family.

"Where is she?" The woman behind the counter was slow and dim as a cow, with the same wide, watery eyes and sagging jowls. She stared through the bullet-proof glass at him, as though the demand had to take its time working through the atoms of the substance that posed as air to get to her ears.

When it did, her hands slowly moved to the worn keyboard in front of the computer; even through the scratched and worn glass, Shane could see her fingers tremble with age.

"Who?" She did not sound as slow and gentle as she looked; surely there was apathy in her voice, but she sounded just as vicious as one might expect a receptionist in LA, any part of LA, to sound, let alone one seated behind the desk at a police station.

"Maya." He huffed and stomped his foot like a horse in frustration as she simply stared at him, the word, the name, still worming its way through the glass, into her ear, down through the canal to her brain.

"Maya who?" she asked, then, and Shane lifted both hands to his face to rub at the burned skin roughly, trying not to scream.

"Maya. She doesn't have a last name."

The woman sighed, lifted her hands from the keyboard. "Everyone's got a last name, honey, whether or not they use it."

He shook his head, biting hard at the inside of his lip, hard enough to taste copper. "She doesn't. She just doesn't. Where is she? They picked her up an hour ago."

"I don't have a Maya in the system, honey," she said. She seemed unaffected, maybe bored, tired of seeing him and people like him.

"She should have been brought in an hour ago. Maybe a little longer."

"What for?" It was barely a question; she could have been asking, idly, how the weather was outside.

He swallowed; he didn't want to say it. "Murder," he said, finally.

Her hands dropped to her lap completely. "No one's been brought in."

He believed her, and stepped away from the counter, hands at his sides. How could that be true, though? He'd seen Maya in cuffs, seen her curled up on herself, in some kind of surrender. The cops had surrounded her, had taken her away, started combing the beach. They had her.

Could they have taken her somewhere else?

He went back outside, tipped his head back and exposed his face fully to the sun. He wanted to go back and punch Louis square in the face, wanted to pitch him into the ocean and kill him once and for all. The old man had nearly drowned once before — why couldn't he follow through this time?

Shane breathed in, and breathed out. That wasn't the solution. That wasn't what Maya wanted.

He started walking, hoping his feet would guide him. He had no idea where the other police stations were, if there was a point in looking. What if they'd taken her out of the city entirely, what if they all died in a car accident on the way there? The number of options was dizzying, and he was already tired, hungry, hot and sick, and, leaning against the side of a building, under an overhang and the shade it afforded him, he closed his eyes, turned his forehead to the brick and tried to think.

"You Levron?"

If he'd dozed off there, standing up, he was rendered wide awake with that name. There was a cop there, another, one he'd not seen before. He was younger, handsome, and his eyes were kind.

"Who are you?" he replied, digging his fingers into the disintegrating brick of the wall.

"We got a call that a missing boy was traced to a pay phone near Venice Beach." The officer smiled, slightly, and Shane realized he wasn't much older than he was, himself.

"You Levron?" he repeated.

Shane nodded, once, and then bolted.

CHAPTER TWENTY-SIX

"Shane."

Her voice was vaporous, as if out of a dream, sing-song and far away. It came from above him, around him, inside him, and he turned his head in one direction, and then the other, trying to gauge its location.

"Shane, you're sick. Don't open your eyes."

There was a silence that was full of sound. It was that sort of silence of in between, under, rather than without, and he sucked in a breath through his mouth, nose clotted and full and aching.

Maya's fingers went to his brow, cold against feverish skin. Water touched his lips, and he swallowed in great gulps, breaking only to suck in the breath of a drowning man before his tongue was snaking out for more.

Gradually, he became aware they were in the cave again, the dampness and the cool familiar though he rarely slept inside it. The cave was where Maya was safe, and he was grateful for it.

Though she'd told him not to, he opened his eyes slowly. It was dark, of course, as it always was, but he could make out variations in it: the blacker tone of the rocks; her smoother, lighter shade hovering above him. He knew her shape well, and his fingers reached up to seek it out, brushing the cool of her hand first, and then the sleek curve of her cheek.

"You need to eat." She did not sound worried, or harried, just that placid calm of unstirred water. Her fingers landed on his lips, stroking the broken and chapped skin there.

"What happened?" His voice was rough and it hurt to speak.

He could see her shadow shake its head, the long tangles of her hair making a rasping noise against her shoulders.

"Sunstroke," she said, and he could almost hear the smile on her voice. "You should know better."

"I couldn't find you," he said, as that was his only answer. He could remember the day before now, racing down the smoggy city streets under the unrelenting sun, his sweat soaking every inch of him. She had vanished off the face of the earth, it seemed, and now the police wanted him too, wanted to uproot him, tear them apart.

But they were back in the cave, like a rewound tape, and she did not fight him as he struggled to sit up. Her hand wound around his arm just above his elbow to help steady him.

"You were arrested." That much was clear.

She made a small noise. "Sort of." Something made of glass was pressed against his hand. "Drink some more. You've been out all night."

He lifted the bottle to his lips; it was sparkling water, and it made his tongue feel fuzzy and alive.

"What's sort of?" he asked, once the bottle was drained.

Another small noise, and he heard the clink of metal against rock. "I left."

"You escaped," he corrected her, as if her knowledge of English had gone a bit askew.

"I left," she countered, and he understood her then, and nodded.

"They're going to come back for you," he said, finding

a place to set the bottle aside. Shane still couldn't see her — there was no light filtering in above them to give his eyes something to acclimate to, use as a reference. He could hear her breathing, though, her hair brushing her shirt and skin, her fingers on rock and sand.

"I know," she said, and, black against black, he could see her shrugging her shoulders. "I know."

His hand sought out hers and, when his fingers curled around hers, he squeezed them. "We can leave."

It was without question that she would protest, but he couldn't let the notion pass him by.

She kissed the back of his hand. "No."

"Why can't we? If you need the water, there's more water, all the way down the coast. We could get to Mexico."

"Shane. Levron." She had only said his real name once, and the sound of it, in her voice, from her lips, made him shiver, and not entirely unpleasantly.

"I can't leave. Not yet."

This was the first time he'd heard a conditional. Though his brain was hung up, a little, on her use of his name, he struggled to retain focus on the conversation, to ignore the rather overwhelming desire to kiss her instead.

"When?" He tried not to sound too desperate, but there was that pulling in his gut that meant a lot of things.

"Not until I'm free." It was simple, sounded simple, but too simple. He groaned a little, recalling he had a second hand and using it to rub at his eyes.

"So it's this little patch of sand, this bit of water?" he asked, after a long moment.

"Yes." The smile was gone from her voice, and she sighed, the sound of water lapping against the shore. "That's how it is. Where you put your feet down is your home."

"And you can't make your feet keep moving?" he asked; he tried not to snap, but it was a struggle. When Maya spoke in puzzles like that, in the spaces in between meanings, Shane couldn't really help the frustration that clawed at the back of his throat.

"Not for us. I made my choice to walk on this beach and, until I'm untied from the ocean, this is where I have to stay."

He found himself laying back against the sand again, directing his gaze up towards the darker black above them. The cave was not big: he couldn't stretch out his legs lying there, nor could he rise to his full height while standing. Right then, though, it felt as though they'd sunk somewhere deep underground when they were there, far from these stories she told, of the police that had had her, however briefly, and the police looking for him, far from Louis and his plans and his hands stinking of bleach.

"So what do we do?" he asked, as if she'd have any answer better than his own.

"We wait."

He lay there, and, eventually, she lay beside him, so that their arms were touching, the line of their legs, and, instinctively, his hand curled around hers and held it. The rough weave of wet yarn, her fingerless gloves, made his palm itch, but he didn't draw away.

Shane had never been a very impatient person, but it was difficult to know what she meant by wait, or how time was passing. He remembered light filtering into the cave, through cracks in the rocks, and wondered if she'd sealed them in. That gave him a brief moment of panic, the idea of a sort of tomb, and he rolled onto his side, close to her, enough to feel her breath on his skin, and calmed.

"How long do we have to wait?" he asked. It felt like it had been a long time already, and his break of the silence was a rock through a window.

She startled, rolled close to him, reached up to trace the contours of his face with her fingertips, as though reading Braille. "I don't know."

Shane sighed, and then he kissed her, as if he had no

other choice. In a way, he did not, and she kissed him back with that same mix of resignation and need, and, in that same spirit, their hands moved clothes away, sodden and sticking to skin, rubbed goosebumps from exposed flesh.

He kissed her neck and her throat, her shoulder, and down the center of her chest, over the fine architecture of her rib cage. Just lower, her belly swelled like a gentle crest, and he stopped there, at the heat that had grown with her, the smoothness of her skin like the oiled pelt of an animal.

"What are we gonna name it?" he asked, after another moment.

They rarely talked about the baby, and not because either of them were scared or sad. Shane was happy, really, something he didn't think he would have expected years back, but it was an abstract concept, a child, something made of him and her, and a name was too solid for something like that.

But, if they were to wait, what else could they talk about? Planning had thrust itself into the forefront of his mind, and now he was cupping the roundness that her body had taken on, the foreign land he'd just started learning turned exotic once more.

She pet the back of his neck, down over his spine and shoulders. "You'd have to give it a name," she said, softly, more like breathing than actual speaking.

He raised his head. "Why me?"

"We don't name things the way you do."

She'd told him that once, and he understood, more emotionally than logically: things had names for communication, to give them weight, but, he knew, she was not like him, and her weight was not his weight.

"You named yourself," he pointed out, smiling in the darkness, hoping she smiled too.

"I did. I don't know that I did a good job."

"It works." It wasn't quite right, really, and he'd thought that from the start: he'd been unable to name her, but, when she finally told him, it seemed like a name from another planet, or picked from a pool. Maya.

"What about my name? Did I do a good job?" he asked.

Maya was quiet for a moment. "I think you did exactly what you needed to do."

More puzzling answers, and he shook his head, kissed the skin of her abdomen right above her navel. Somewhere under there was a child developing, someone they'd made, something mysterious and fantastical, and he was given the responsibility to name it.

"I guess he — she — can always change it if it doesn't like it, right?" he mused.

Her fingers pinched his earlobe gently.

"Why would you want it to do that?" she said, voice like water. "Wouldn't you want it to have the right name, so it never feels like it has to change it? Like she's wearing something that doesn't fit?"

Shane considered that. "How important is that? Who feels that bad about their name?" His real name, Levron, had just been that: a name, something his mother came up with because that's what mothers did.

"Lots of people," Maya replied. "People who go through life wondering what is wrong with them, that they're not happy, but for no real reason. They have love, and success, and there's always something gnawing at them. And, you know, it could be a name, something trapping them inside themselves, making it impossible to ever really see anything clearly — the sky, the ocean. Everything is covered by... by this sort of sheet, thin, but opaque. They're never really themselves because they've never been free."

She spoke of freedom a lot, moreso over the past few weeks, and Shane was quiet, listening to her words, trying to absorb them, getting lost in the cadence instead.

"The wrong name is a curse," she said, exhaling hard enough that her stomach rose against his hands; an image of a baby, turning and swimming deep inside her, flashed through his mind.

"I'll think about it," he said. It sounded so daunting, this task, insuring his child was not cursed from the start.

Her thumbs went under his chin, stroked the soft, vulnerable flesh there.

"You'll do a good job," she said, softly. In that position, her hands were nearly wound around his neck and, should she choose, she could have easily throttled him.

"I'll do my best," he replied, without fear of her hands, of her power, of her in any way.

It was easy to love Maya, to want to have those fingers on your skin, to hear her voice in your ear. She knew it was easy, too easy; wonderfully easy. She held his head like that for another moment, and released it, dragging her thumbs along his cheeks, full and warm.

"Of course you will," she whispered. "Of course."

CHAPTER TWENTY-SEVEN

They waited, like moles, hidden from the world. Shane didn't know how Maya did it, how she had found the spot in that shallow line of rocks, but the cave was sort of big enough for the both of them, and he heard no one climb over, or even walk near. When the tide moved out, there was just a kind of charged silence - though, he could admit, it was probably just him.

Frequently, he found himself holding his breath only when he became dizzy from lack of oxygen. His muscles still ached from the sunstroke, and ached some more from being in such a cramped space with no way to stretch them all at once. He lifted one arm up and touched the rough ceiling of the cave, eased his shoulder out, spread his fingers, and then repeated the maneuver with his other arm, hand and shoulder. Backed up against the wall, he stretched his legs, one at a time, into a crevice, wedging his toes there, tipping them forward to ease his ankle, to stretch the muscles of his calves, up to his knee, and thigh.

Maya did not do the same. She stayed carefully curled, feet under her behind, arms around the jutting curve of her belly. The baby had just started kicking, she said, flutters like a fish tail and Shane wondered if it would have a tail, be born slippery like a fish, the same shimmering scales as its mother, with his skin underneath.

They stayed quiet, mostly, and touched often. Maya

peeled away her gloves and slipped her glossy fingers along his, and they held hands for hours, maybe days, as Shane lost track, his body unsure of night or day, but slipping into sleep often, contorted and tired.

There was food, and he didn't know where she got it, but it was shoved into another crevice at the back of the cave: water, and some bags of things, a few hard oranges. There were so many things he couldn't quite ask about, didn't want to, but they shared the fruit, her tiny delicate bites, and he rationed his intake of the chips, multigrain, and tasting of cheese powder.

"How long?" he asked, but only once, daily, though it could have been hourly. Maya had a sort of infinite patience, and shook her head, petting the bone behind his ear with her fingertips.

"I don't know."

It was easy to be driven mad in the dark, though Maya didn't seem to be afraid, or bothered in any fashion. Shane would have paced had there been the room, and so he wiggled his feet, and hands, until, finally, one day, he rubbed his face roughly with a sigh that sounded somewhat like a muffled scream.

"We should look," he announced. He could feel her shift beside him, drawing her hands over her stomach, the fabric of her shirt, always damp, making a silken noise against her skin.

"Why?" She didn't sound afraid.

"Because I can't stand it much longer," he replied, frustration already back at the back of his throat, coloring his words. "Because this is getting pointless. We can't stay in here forever."

He could feel her gaze in the dark: of course she could, maybe she had before. But Shane was human, and needed the light, and thought, with that inkling of claustrophobic insanity, that the baby would too.

"I'm going to check," he said, and didn't wait for her

response. Shane rose up on his knees and felt for the rocks he knew were loose, and would move aside for him to, at the very least, poke his head out, and look at the world.

Maya didn't stop him. She was not cowering, but she did not move, staying in the spot of the cave that the light would not reach, watching him with her ocean eyes. She'd never been much of a speaker, and Shane understood now, maybe, where the legend of the Little Mermaid came from, with her stolen voice and eyes older than the earth.

He wasn't looking at her, though: he was pushing the rocks away, carefully, one at a time so that, from the outside, the movement was not obvious. He couldn't imagine anyone, save Louis, against the outcropping of rocks, but, even in his sort of stir-crazy mind, he knew to be careful.

Little by little, light appeared, and, finally, he had a hole large enough to put his head and shoulders through. He was almost panting with the anticipation, with that watery grey light of a cold morning, but he forced himself to be calm, to move slowly, and, once his eyes adjusted to the light, he was glad he did.

The beach was covered in cops. There were lines of bright yellow tape drawn along trees and, closer to the water, stakes sunk into the sand. There were vehicles driven down to the line, and holes dug, tables set up. Most of the cops were uniformed, but, from the rocks, Shane could make out ones in waders, scuba suits, dragging nets, examining refuse.

He dropped back into the cave, breathing hard. Maya was still watching him.

"They came, didn't they?" She didn't sound surprised, still, or afraid. She stated it with so little emotion, Shane almost wanted to shake her, just to see some sort of realization, even fear, in her eyes.

"The beach is crawling with police," he told her, tongue thick and difficult to work. He could feel his pulse at his wrists and in his throat, and the taste in his mouth was almost like he was swallowing blood with every beat of his heart.

Maya nodded, and reached out a hand to him. After a moment's hesitation, he took it, and helped her to her feet.

She didn't really need the assistance, but she held onto his hand anyway, lifting up on her toes to poke just the very top of her head out of the hole to squint between the rocks and down the beach.

He didn't know if she was simply confirming, counting, or what, and, after another minute, he gave her hand a nervous tug.

Maya glanced down at him. "I think they're looking for you," she said, softly, her eyebrows knit together.

In a flash, Shane remembered the police officer asking his name, his real name, and recalled the look in the young man's eyes. He hadn't thought of the repercussions of giving his mother his whereabouts, or that anyone would respond with her same sense of urgency.

He sunk to the sand, eyes that had been so desperate for something to feast themselves upon now unfocused on the trampled soil beneath them. He could hear the incessant dripping of water between the rocks once more, but, now, couldn't make himself care.

"And what if they don't find me?" he asked, finally.

She joined him, though she squatted, unable to quite bend towards him the way she was used to, but sliding her hands up over his shoulders anyway, holding him in place.

"They're looking for me too. Even more if you've disappeared."

He licked at his lips. "What if I turn myself in?" he offered, raising his eyebrows. "Or, you know, made 'em run after me? Called my mom again, told her I'm going to, like, Las Vegas or something."

She didn't quite understand, her giant eyes blinking rapidly.

Shane continued: "You know, so you'd have time to

run."

Again, it was useless, beating his head against a brick wall. Maya shook her head. "You know I can't."

"But you have to!" he finally exploded, though he was aware enough not to raise his voice. The effect was the same, though, and her shoulders curled slightly.

"You know I can't. It's not possible."

"Just for a little while," he pleaded. "Just long enough for them to go after me. Until I'm eighteen. I'm almost there."

"Levron," she breathed out, her face etched with pain, confusion, an ancient sort of weariness. "This is where I'm tied, until I can be freed."

"How, though?" His jaw hurt, he was clenching it so hard. "You've tried, you have. You — you gave those guys to the ocean, you did what you thought would do it."

She licked at her lips, pink on pink, hands dropping to her knees. "I was wrong."

"But what's right?" he demanded, almost trembling with the combine panic and fear and love. "How are we supposed to figure it out if we're just trapped here?"

Maya shrugged and looked away again, into the blackness of the cave, as though she could see something he could not. Shane exhaled and tipped his chin up and looked towards the sky, grey and solid above them.

"I'm going out," he announced, and he could feel her startle next to him, though she did not reach for him again.

"They'll catch you," she said, softly, mournfully.

"They can't catch me," he disagreed, and then climbed up out of the cave and into the world once more.

CHAPTER TWENTY-EIGHT

Shane barely took a breath of the fresh air before hands clamped around his shoulders and yanked him backwards.

He was airborne for a split second, but it felt like hours. The sky was a flat grey, and so there was a strange illusion of floating rather than falling. When he hit the ground, he was surprised in more ways than one.

"Give it up."

He knew it was Louis before his vision managed to right itself. He blinked up at the man who was as grey and flat and unmoving as the sky, looking more grizzled as the weeks had eaten away at them both.

Now, though, he saw a tired, sad old man and Shane sighed, struggling to his feet.

"Get over it," he muttered, but Louis shoved him back to the sand, surprisingly strong.

"They're looking for you, boy," he spat, as if Shane didn't know.

He sighed. "I know. I'm going to show them I'm alive. So they'll leave Maya alone."

Louis snorted; it sounded dry and painful, and he swiped at his nose, leaving a black streak over his fingers and the back of his hand. It only took a moment for Shane to register it was blood, and stare at him anew.

"They're not looking for your body, Levron." His voice was mocking and Shane flinched. "They're looking for you."

He couldn't quite understand the difference, and blinked like a cow several times, Louis breaking into a horrible cackle.

"She turned it on you!" he announced, throwing up his hands, the atrophied one and the one smeared with blood. "How do you think she got away?"

Shane opened his mouth, closed it. He'd not thought to ask Maya how she went from cuffed and surrounded by police to rescuing him and hiding out in the cave. It wasn't a question in his mind: it was magical, like her, like everything about what had happened to him since that first night he saw her face.

Louis nodded, almost maniacally, his head bobbing on his spindly neck. He looked ancient in the watery light, and Shane could smell rain on the air, a storm on its way.

"She blamed you, boy." The man's whole body was jittery, as if he was just barely able to keep it from flying apart. "Told them you did it. That's why she's hiding you. They ain't gonna send a kid three weeks off his eighteenth birthday back to his mama."

Louis was speaking in a way that Shane had never heard, not from him, and he found himself taking a step back, stumbling over the smaller, hidden rocks, to fall against the larger ones. The cave was encased somewhere in there, though Shane could never really figure out how: the line of boulders wasn't tall or wide enough to contain the space, even as small as it was.

"The cop knew my name," Shane countered, though his voice wavered.

"So does she, don't she?" Louis licked his lips; a tooth was missing where it hadn't been before, and the sight was shocking for some reason, like a Jack-o-Lantern out at the wrong time of year.

"Names are dangerous."

Maya's words from Louis' mouth made Shane's body

shudder, hard, one large movement that ground his spine against the jagged portion of the rocks.

Names were dangerous, she'd told him that, with those big, sad eyes, eyes that were the ocean, never really a color and all of them at once, and he'd believed her, always believed her—

"No." His voice was chocked, but his hands balled into fists at his thighs. "You're just pissed. You're crazy. She's not trying to get me blamed."

"You think they're doing this on no evidence?" Louis' hand swept in the direction of the cops who were sweeping the other side of the beach, just out of sight behind the rocks. "You think she didn't tell them where bodies might be found?"

Shane shook his head. "She told them they went out in the ocean. She didn't lie."

"And they let her go because that was nice of her?" He cackled again, a wild, high sound, making Shane flinch.

"She just… escaped." Shane swallowed, fighting to keep that sense of conviction surging through his veins. It was difficult.

"She got freed," Louis argued, widening his eyes, holding his hands up, fingers spread. "She used you for her freedom. Just like she did Trey, and Donovan, and all the rest."

The accusation struck him, but it did not sting. It didn't stick, either, slithering away, afraid. Shane could feel the courage inside him again, solidifying his bones.

"Not you." His gaze was unwavering on Louis. "But not you."

Louis went rigid: Shane knew he was right, knew that Louis, though he'd loved her like all of them did, every last one of them, she'd had no reason to give him up, let him go. She'd done nothing to save him from the wave that knocked him from his board, nearly drowned him, and done nothing to set him free.

"She failed," the man said, after a minute, two, while

the sound of the ocean had begun to rise behind him, the grey on the horizon growing darker, clustering.

"She tried to kill me too, but I didn't let her."

"You wanted her to take you and she wouldn't," Shane shot back, before Louis had even gotten all the words out of his thin, angry mouth.

"You wanted to be special, but you're not. You're just like the rest of us. Just like me."

Did it hurt to admit? A bit like poison pumped directly into his heart, but Shane was so sure of his words, he remained upright, staring down the older man, challenging him to fight back against that truth.

Louis stayed stiff, hard, a sort of long-harbored rage making it impossible to blow him down that easily.

"She doesn't love you, boy," he said then, glowering. "She doesn't love anything but that ocean."

"Same as you." Shane pushed away from the rocks, steady on his feet despite the fatigue, the starvation, the sand giving under them both. "Same as me. The ocean is our home and we're not special. We're not special."

The wind was blowing the storm in, and his last words were shouted over the sound of it, like a freight train barreling in over the water. His eyes watered with the force of it, but he stood his ground, jeans flapping, wet, around his ankles.

While the sky had been grey, there was no indication where the storm had come from. On the other side of the rocks, people gathered up their towels and umbrellas as quickly as they could while, further down the beach, the police were shutting down their investigation due to the waves that were now tall and crashing, black and white and foaming. It felt like hurricane weather, there on the west coast, and that was never good, and never something to fuck around with.

Shane remained where he was. Something about the gathering storm, the cold wind, the strange light after so many days of darkness, made him feel strong, stronger than Louis, taller and bigger and more powerful.

The man glared at Shane, though, continued to, before, in the blink of an eye, he turned and dashed in the direction of the water.

Shane stared after him, stunned, for a long moment. Then he screamed: "Maya!"

He needn't have called for her: she was already standing atop the rocks, like a visage, silver and grey and white and black, all the colors, hair whipping back from her face with the force of the wind. He looked up at her for a long moment before breaking into a run himself, kicking off his shoes and tearing his hoodie from his body.

Louis hit the water before him, down further as the tide rolled out, like a great beast sucking in a breath. Shane's feet sunk into the sand as he ran, and the giant continued pulling in that murky breath, exhaling just as the ground beneath him dampened.

The wave surged up over his head and crashed down, and he vanished from view.

CHAPTER TWENTY-NINE

Under the water, the sound of the storm all but disappeared. It was a strange sort of silence, one that was not silent at all, but thick and cold— warm, too, moving ceaselessly. It was a suspension of time, something like flying through the air; the first moment dunked under the surface hanging for what felt like eons, an embrace there was no way out of, and rarely a desire to try.

The ocean was restless, but, under the waves, it was calm, almost to a point of apathy. It was living, but it was not, and it had a purpose, a drive, yet no horse in the race — it did not intend for anyone to suffer, yet did not care if it caused the suffering. It was overwhelming, enormous, weighted and weightless.

Maya stood on the rocks, frozen. Her clothes stuck to her like a second skin, damp already from the cave, growing wet with the rain that blew in from the roiling clouds overhead. She did not feel the cold, even as the skin of her arms pebbled and her body shook. Her eyes watered as she would not blink, couldn't blink, couldn't look away from the water.

The storm was bearing down on the beach, and the police hurriedly dragged their tents into vans, raced inside the vehicles against the weather. Sunbathers and swimmers had dashed in the direction of the shops and restaurants for refuge, and even the surfers had come up shore, the waves choppy and violent. The storm seemed to have some kind of emotion, and seemed intent on taking it out on the scrap of land named Venice.

Maya's hair was like whips against her face and back, and she could feel the child inside her stirring, as though it knew what was happening outside its mother's body. Maya felt unsteady and small just then, a sensation that was almost completely foreign to her: unsteady and small and scared, and her eyes stayed locked on the spot where Shane had disappeared, and the area beyond it, out over the raging ocean.

A sound rose in her throat, high and panicked, when a dark spot appeared. She scrambled like a mountain goat over the rocks, closer to where the water was dashing up upon them, stumbling and catching herself on her gloved palms; the rocks bit into her hands anyway.

"Shane!" Maya had never screamed in her life, and her voice was something like the wind, an audible bolt of lightning, the tearing of the sky. "Shane!"

Thunder rolled overhead: not a clap but a growl, drawn-out and lingering. Maya rocked onto her bloodied and painful palms, as though thrusting her body forward those few inches would send her voice further. "Shane!"

He did not hear her, his head bobbing just above water. He was thrashing against the waves, the undertow, and she could see flashes of his dark arms, stark against the water gone white, as he made some crude attempt at strokes, as though those would move him through the water.

He couldn't swim. Maya knew this, she always knew this: it was something in the composition of these humans, how they were made of so much water and yet fought it so hard. Shane loved the water, yearned for it, and he could not swim.

"Shane!" she screamed again, tears running down her face. Her throat was raw and ragged, and she swallowed, the saltiness burning as it went down. It felt as though there were strips of torn skin there, swollen and catching on her breaths, and she coughed against them, bowing her head against the rain, struggling to catch her breath.

When she looked up again, Shane had vanished. The journey to her feet took too long, and she scraped her knees, tearing the tightly-woven fabric of her jeans as she did so. Without much thought, she dashed the last few feet of rocks, and jumped onto the sand, jarring her hard enough to dash her teeth together and send a ringing pain through her skull. She wavered, steadied herself, and ran to the waterline, jumping up on her toes, screaming his name against the wind.

She could see him again, just the top of his head, not his arms, now, and he was struggling. She dashed forward, and then fell back, almost by an unseen hand. It knocked her back hard enough that she stumbled, and fell, sprawling on the wet sand so that her head fell back and she was looking up at the angry sky.

Maya couldn't breathe. She didn't want to. There was nothing she could do.

Still, she struggled to sit up, pushing her hands against the ground to find a way to standing once more. She could see Shane out in the water, struggling with his load: Louis. Somehow he had found that miserable old man under the churning water and, despite his limited ability, was trying to drag him in.

She could almost feel his panic, the way the water stung his lips and went up his nose. Louis was slack, greyed head barely bobbing above the waterline and, for a hateful second, she wished he'd let him go, find a way against the storm, and come back to her. Leave that crazed asshole to the fate he seemed to desire so much, had been begging for since he first found a surfboard. But she couldn't hold the thought long, feeling her heart beating in her feet, nails digging into her aching palms.

The water forced Shane down, over and over, but sheer will and determination kept him from letting it drag him down. Despite the cold hands of the undertow, he inched closer to shore.

The rain beat down on his head, and it was only through instinct that he knew he was headed in the right direction. He had no idea if Louis was alive or dead: the old coot had fought at first, and then was either overwhelmed or knocked out, or died, hell, and hung limp in Shane's right arm, the weight of his body almost harder to struggle with than the water and storm.

He kicked and kicked, and thought nothing about the fact that he could not swim, that he'd never been in the ocean past his ankles before. He didn't know why he'd gone in after Louis except for what he'd said, what he believed: they weren't special. Louis' death would do nothing for him, would prove nothing about Maya, and would not fix what had been taken from him all those years ago. They were just players, just bits and pieces of the universe, collateral that would not prevent the cogs from moving, from keeping the whole damned machine running into eternity and beyond.

Shane kicked, and pushed as hard as he could, even as his grip continued to slip on Louis. He grit his teeth and kicked, and then another giant wave came over them both and tore them apart.

Maya was on her feet, and this time she managed to tear into the water, slicing through the opposing current without effort, up to her hips. Her hands went to her belly, over the top, over where her child — suddenly a girl, she knew without question — turned and fluttered within.

She stood, and she looked up at the sky, and before she could look back out at the water, search for Shane's dark head, Louis' body threw the both of them back onto the beach.

The old man was blue, but alive, wheezing ever so slightly. Maya hooked her hands under his arms and dragged him up the beach, out of the reach of the enormous waves. His clothes were water-logged and filled with sand, as though he'd had a moment to scoop handfuls into his pockets to weight him down. She tipped his head up, and he spit up water, coughed, and sagged against the ground.

She dropped him there, back up on her feet. She was just about to run again when she felt a tear through her soul.

"No." Her lips barely moved, and no sound came out. Not until the next, when she screamed, louder than before, louder than the sudden clap of thunder and the wave that smacked down against the shore: "No!"

A moment before, she had tasted the water, rippling down her throat, up her nose, had felt his heart slamming with hers, driving the beat incessantly. Now she couldn't, now it was gone.

She fell down hard on her knees, hands going to the ground, grabbing at the sand, flinging it at the ocean. She screamed, but there were no words. She screamed, but nothing, no one, answered.

The thunder abruptly stopped, and Maya collapsed against the sand. She kept her eyes closed and nose pressed to the grains for a minute, two, ten hours, a year. She counted as high as she could with every breath, and then back again.

The storm rolled back out to sea. When Maya lifted her head, the clouds overhead were already breaking up, and she could see the watery light of the sun filtering through. It felt like she was underwater once more, like she was looking up at the sky through the thin layer, the barrier between worlds.

Instinctively, her fingers went to her neck, where the skin was smooth. She peeled away her gloves to find her hands pale and covered in goose bumps. Then her shirt, her jeans; Maya stood naked on the beach, wearing a whole new body.

There was a chill she had never felt before, and her

arms hugged her bare frame. She could feel her hair wet against her back, and the grains of sand under her feet, shifting with every breath. She was – suddenly, altogether, inexplicably - free.

EPILOGUE

She could not give birth in the ocean as her mother had done, and so she had her baby in the county hospital, hissing at the nurses who came near her with needles bound for her spine.

She writhed and spit and screamed under their machines, but, at the end, a baby girl was laid upon her chest, with cocoa-colored skin and slow blinking eyes. Her hands were clutched in fists like nuts and her mouth was like a pink rosebud, closed over all her secrets.

Maya had never ridden on a bus, or in any vehicle besides the police car months before, and it was strange and entertaining. She found she liked the sensation of rolling down the highway at a fast clip, the scenery outside the windows all but a blur of lights and darkness, dirt and wind.

She had never left the beach, of course, and the flatness the world took on kept her plastered to the glass in a way the rest of the passengers seemed to take for granted. The landscape was bland and long, but her eyes followed every bump in the dirt, every tuft of grass that waved in the wind. The baby rested against her chest, her cheek downy soft, breaths like feathers. They were discovering the world together.

Shane had had nearly four thousand dollars in the boot he'd dropped on the beach as he ran into the water. Maya was unsure if she should take it but, ultimately did, sliding it into the pocket of the jeans that were wet and shrunken against her skin, dashing away from Louis as he woke on the sand.

She didn't know why he had the money, but that it was there, and hers now. She slid it across the counter at the bus station for a ticket, for the place he'd only talked about a few times, the place where he was born. Home.

The other passengers were kind, and when the day switched places with the night, the woman riding next to her let her put the armrest down so the baby was supported in the crook of her elbow. That way, Maya could rest her forehead against the glass and flit in and out of sleep.

She dreamed of the beach, of Shane, of the ocean, dark and bottomless. There was a part of her that missed that home, but it was not her blood, not her heartbeat, any longer. His death had freed her.

She'd stayed on the beach all night, watching the police come back, setting up their van and tents, lights to illuminate the night. They were searching for other bodies they wouldn't find, and Shane's as well, and she stayed curled on the sand, naked but for the hair down her back.

Louis was out for hours, and stirred only once. She placed her hand over his eyes and listened to him breathe, but it wasn't enough. She pulled her wet clothes on, found Shane's discarded ones, and disappeared into the slowly-gathering crowds on the boardwalk.

She collected her skates from the locker, Shane's backpack from another one. Inside was a book, pairs of socks, a card from a seaside shop. She carried this with her and, at the hospital, they dressed the baby in a tiny shirt the sleeves of which hung over her balled fists, and Maya bought a pack of diapers with some of the cash from the boot, and carefully wrapped her tiny daughter's body with them.

The miles rolled on outside her window, and the baby woke and slept with her, latched onto her breast with that secretive rosebud mouth. Her daughter was quiet and calm, with eyes older than herself, older than the world, and Maya felt both overwhelmed with the responsibility of such a creature, and a love that felt as natural to her as breathing.

They were getting low on diapers when the bus finally rolled into the depot, the destination she'd marked on the map in her mind. She gathered up the backpack, the hoodie and boots, the skates she kept tied together so she could throw them over her opposite shoulder. Maya cradled the baby between her breasts and carried her down the steps carefully, into the heat of the Indian summer, gazing around for something, anything, familiar.

The woman had his face, the same way the baby did, and they moved towards one another without even noticing. The woman looked older than she expected, with the tired expression of someone who had had her world dashed too many times. She gazed down at the baby with a lump in her throat.

"This her?" she asked, softly, looking up at Maya with a trembling lip, as though she couldn't let herself believe it was true just yet.

Maya nodded, and held her bundle of a daughter out to her grandmother. "This is her."

The woman took the baby into her arms, gaze locking with the prematurely old one of the infant. "What's her name?" she asked, unable to tear her eyes away.

Maya sucked in her breath, biting the soft skin of the inside of her lips with the edges of her teeth. "Shane," she told her, name like a whisper.

"Shane," the grandmother repeated, lifting her hand to trace the curve of the baby's cheek with her finger. Shane's eyes were just like Levron's as a baby, already holding so much inside them. "Hi, there, Shane. I'm your grandmamma."

Maya smiled, and she rolled up on her toes. The ocean was far away. She was free.

AT THE EDGE OF THE WORLD

ABOUT THE AUTHOR

Lorrie Colin Spoering has a degree in English writing from University of Colorado, and a lesser degree in sarcasm earned from the days of yore on AOL. A storyteller since she started talking, she now spends her days writing, reading and contemplating the universe through various pop culture lenses.

A native of Denver, the feral daughter of two teachers, she now lives with her husband, two children and entirely too many pets. Her online home is located at www.lcspoering.com.

After Life Lessons is a women's fiction drama, featuring some zombies, grief, and tentative love.

After months of struggling south to escape the zombie-infested remains of New York, a snowstorm traps 23-year old artist, Emily, and her son in an abandoned gas station. Starving and desperate, they encounter Aaron, an Army medic on a mission of his own, who offers them a ride to ease the journey.

The road is a long and dangerous place to travel, and every day brings a new threat. But fear and adrenaline also drive the two closer together; they find laughter and a budding attraction that starts to thaw at their numb and deadened feelings. And that's when the pain really starts to hit, when places long thought lost prickle back to life. Eventually, they will have to fight not just for survival, but for a future together, or their broken world will swallow them whole.

This novel contains language some might find offensive, some gore and situations of a sexual nature. Reader's discretion is advised.

Medieval Romantic Fantasy with a Paranormal Twist!

Withdrawn and with a reputation for her strange, eccentric ways, young Lady Moira Rochmond is old to be unwed. Rumors say, she has been seen barefoot in the orchard, is awake all night in moon-struck rambles and sleeps all day. Some will even claim her ghostly pallor and aloof manner are signs of illness, of a curse or insanity.

The hopes of the peaceful succession to her father's fief lie in an advantageous marriage. When a suitor does show interest, her family pushes for a decision.

Almost resigned to the fact that she has no choice but to play the part she has been given in life, Moira is faced with Owain. A member of the mysterious Blaidyn creatures and a new guard in her father's castle, he is specifically tasked to keep her safe. He is different from other people she knows and when one night under the full moon, she makes the acquaintance of the wolf who shares Owain's soul, her life starts to change and to unravel.

Lakeside Series, #1

EXCLUSIVE PREVIEW
A TASTE OF WINTER:
LAKESIDE #2
BY LAILA BLAKE

The cottage loomed in the distance like a crouching animal, like a tortoise—its shell covered in moss and dirt and snow. The roof had long started to slump under its weight but no one had come to repair it. Nobody ever came here—it was too deep in the forest, too far away from any trodden path.

Maeve stood still after the long walk, watching the quiet place. It looked abandoned, but she still felt the life inside, as she always had. She took a deep breath as though to settle herself in her disguise. The aging skin felt too soft around her tired bones, the white hair was brittle under her gnarly fingers. The mask had aged over the years in a way Maeve never would.

Finally, her steps led her down a narrow dirt path, past an ill-kept vegetable patch and a small outhouse. There was a well and a chicken coop, the only voices in the air came from there, high and excited among the beating of stunted wings.

She knocked on the door. It was courtesy more than anything. Inside, she heard a commotion: the clatter of a mug, a worried groan, the gentle hushing of a female voice.

The dull, watery eyes of Maeve's disguise filled with sorrow and again, she sucked a deep breath into her lungs. It tasted like snow and bark and memories.

Finally, Alma opened the door. She was middle-aged but looked prematurely older. The initial note of worry or suspicion on her face gave way to a relieved hint of a smile.

"Oh, it's you. Good day, ma'am," she stepped out of the way and Maeve entered undeterred. The inside smelled musty—like sweat and piss. It was an old smell, the bouquet of those last odors humans emitted when their bodies rotted around their still beating hearts. The Fae shuddered despite her long years among humans and breathed in through her mouth instead.

"How is he?" Maeve asked, looking around. She couldn't see anyone else in the room but she knew he was there. She smelled him, she heard him breathing, she felt his heart beat fast and hard.

Alma followed Maeve's gaze and then shrugged. "'e's not been doin' well, Ma'am. The normal aches and pains, but... bad dreams. Bad dreams even when 'e's awake, Ma'am."

Maeve could see her faltering and finally look away and it made her wonder what things Ronan rambled about in his panic stricken mind. They were infecting the woman, she could see that. She had been young when Maeve had first hired her—not beautiful or rich enough to marry well. She'd been grateful for the position, but Maeve saw the exhaustion in her eyes now. It wasn't physical. Ronan's affliction simply seemed too much for a human mind to bear in the long run, so dark and hopeless and lonely.

She put her hand on Alma's shoulder, squeezed it gently and allowed a little warmth to flow. It was not quite magic, a trick even some humans could learn but it came easily to Fae. The relief in the woman's face was slow but noticeable and, tenderly, Maeve moved her onto a chair.

She placed a leather satchel of coins there and next to it, she emptied her backpack. Some meat, smoked or salted to make it last, a sack of wheat, a loaf of cheese. She always tried to bring something at least.

"I'm going to go check on him," Maeve told the woman who was still sitting there with a relaxed and far-away look on her face. It was better than the haunted quality of before and Maeve felt marginally less guilty as she left her there and entered the only other room in the small cottage.

It housed a bed, a wardrobe, and the remains of a lyre that looked like it had been smashed too many times to repair on an otherwise empty writing desk. Her chest ached with leaden memories.

"Ronan?" she said quietly. She walked around the bed with careful, deliberate steps until she saw him there, hunched in the narrow space between the bed and the wall, his spotty, wrinkled hands pushed in front of his face, his stringy white hair a mess. "Ronan, it is I. Maeve. You remember me, don't you?"

She watched him closely, watched his shivering hands and the way his chest rung with his fearful groan. It was true, he hadn't been doing well.

"I'm sorry I haven't been here in so long," she went on, daintily sitting down on bed. It smelled foul in her sensitive nose, like the man, like the house. "But I'm here now. I'm here now, Ronan. You can look at me, I won't hurt you, I will never hurt you."

He let his shaking hands sink, slowly. They moved with the debilitating sense of age that had strung itself through his every muscle, his every bone. Grief cut her, like a blade. It was his beautiful, familiar face, hidden behind wrinkles and loose flesh, and the insanity that had eroded all the expressions that had once defined him. A mere twenty years ago, he had been a strapping man, strong and independent—with a rebel's heart and a gentle soul. He had aged much too fast.

He whimpered again and, in one fluid motion, Maeve knelt in front of him. She took his hands in hers and kissed first one palm, then the other. His skin was loose, sallow and salty. Salty like the tear that ran down her cheek.

"It's me, Ronan, your wife," she repeated, more passionately. "You know me, I know you know me..." she stopped and breathed in deeply before she gathered herself.

"Come on, I'll help you up. I brought the cheese you like."

"Cheese," he repeated in the cadence of a child and Maeve nodded.

"Cheese. The one you like."

***

"What happened to him?" Maeve asked when he sat at the table and she stood off to the side with his nurse. She had cut some cheese into broad chunks and watched him cramming them into his mouth. He put one on his flat palm, then quickly closed his fist around it and only opened it a fraction of an inch in front of his lips, where he pushed it hard and fast as though afraid someone might take it away at the last minute. It broke her heart all over again.

"'e's been getting worse for a long time, M'am," was the sad and quiet answer. "You knew that... ye told me 'e wouldn't get better."

Maeve nodded. She fought down a lump in her throat and finally averted her eyes. Watching him like that, it seemed indecent on a most primal level. Indecency was a human term that she had rarely been able to fill with meaning but there it was. It seemed indecent to watch a once strong and healthy and beautiful man down in the mud of insanity, fallen so low.

"'e won't make it much longer, I don't think," Alma

said quietly after a while, watching Maeve's glance and then quickly looking down at her woolen slippers. Mice had gnawed holes in them and they had taken on the general state of dust and disrepair of the house. Once her charge died, the woman would have nothing. Maeve knew that and she loathed the responsibility for another human life.

She nodded in the end, eyes back on the man she still loved, despite everything. She was Fae, and Fae were not fickle in their affections.

"Tell me," she finally said, rubbing her own arms in a protective gesture, "about all of it."

Alma stepped from one foot to the other. Finally, she reached for a kettle and filled it with water from a bucket that had seen better days.

"'is eyes are not what they once were," she said once her fingers and hands were distracted and she didn't feel so watched by the strong woman who'd hired her so many years ago. Even now there was something fearful about her. "I reckon, that's why 'e scares so easily. 'e sees them shadows everywhere."

Maeve nodded, pain etched in the artificial lines between her brows.

"'e don't sleep 'nuff neither. Nightmares." She stopped, for a moment, and both women watched the old man who was now inspecting a piece of cheese all too closely with a worried look on his face. Suddenly, he bellowed out a scream and flung it against the wall—where it bounced off once and then fell to the floor. The women jumped but it was Maeve who hurried to his side. She sank to her knees and pulled his hands into her own.

"Hush, my love..." she whispered. There was warmth in her voice and she layered it with a hint of magic. It wasn't something she often risked especially in her hidden cottage but she couldn't watch him suffer like that. Almost instantly, his face relaxed, and he exhaled a deep breath. Tension flowed from his chest and shoulders.

"There was... something in the cheese," he explained

falteringly. Maeve nodded; she squeezed his hands and kissed his knuckles before she got to her feet again.

"It was small and dark," he babbled on, his eyes wide and fearful but not out-right panic stricken. "It moved. It moved... it tried to creepy-crawl into my head... through my eyes and through my ears. It was a dark thing. A dark thing."

"Nightmares." His nurse repeated. She had come up behind Moira and was now quickly moving the remaining cheese off the table, saving it from Ronan's still massive hands. "Sometimes, sometimes 'e cries and whimpers 'e's so afraid to go to sleep. An' who can blame 'im poor soul with things like that in 'is head?"

Maeve didn't disagree, she didn't have the strength for much of anything. She just stood there, gently running her hand over his gray head as though any of that could soothe the darkness inside it. After a while, he seemed to curl inward and against her touch and Maeve kissed his hair and held him tight.

"I'll take him outside into the snow for a little bit," she finally informed the other woman and went to find the heavy moth-eaten coat in a chest. "It's sunny and beautiful."

Alma looked skeptical, but then she held her tongue and burrowed through a drawer for a knitted scarf instead. More docile now, Ronan got to unsteady feet when she asked. Maeve took his arm with that same air of tenderness with which she'd kissed his neck and rubbed the worries out of his back all those years ago.

***

"I met her, you know?" Maeve asked the old man who was looking around the bright snow with the eyes of a child. Maeve knew he wasn't really listening, but it didn't seem to matter. "Moira," she clarified, "our little girl."

There was no answer from the man who just walked next to her, clutching her arm unusually tightly. Maeve blinked and allowed herself to look out over the fresh snow. It glittered in the afternoon sun that reached the clearing. The beauty seemed lost on the man she loved however, and she gently pushed her lips against his shoulder.

"She is beautiful," she told him then, trying to smile. "She has your nose, and when she's skeptical... her mouth makes those little wrinkles just like yours."

Sniffing, she ran her free hand through her white hair, still shivering at the alien sensation of the paper-thin, brittle strands where she was supposed to share Moira's bright and vivacious mass of red curls.

"I just thought you should know—that our daughter is healthy and strong and beautiful. And..." Maeve stopped, her feet halted as well and she gently turned her torso towards Ronan's so that they were facing each other.

"She's in love," she whispered, eyes glinting a little with unshed tears. "We did good, you hear me, we did that for her. We saved her... you... you saved our daughter. It's not... all of it, it... it hasn't been for naught."

Ronan stared down at her, his liquid blue eyes not understanding. He looked terrible, worse here in the light and it broke Maeve's heart all over again. His hair was unwashed, his beard badly shaven, he looked tired and afraid and confused and like he'd skipped some meals. She breathed him in deeply again but instead of the human and spicy musk she still remembered like the first day, all she smelled were the vague remnants of urine, feces and fear. It hadn't been for naught, she knew that now, but the price still had been high. So very high.

"Do you really not remember?" she asked again. This time she brought her hand up to cup his stubbly old cheek. It hurt, selfishly, ungratefully, it hurt more that Maeve was able to weather. Just for a moment, she wanted to hit him, slap him, shake him and squeeze the true Ronan out of him. He had to be in there somewhere and there had to be something she could do. Her fingers tightened on his cheek. The old man whimpered, fear entered his eyes and he backed away.

"I'm sorry!" Maeve uttered immediately, reaching for his hand. "I'm sorry, I'm so sorry... please, I... just remember me. Just once, please Ronan..."

Again, she laced her passionate plea with a hint of magic. Just as much as she dared. She still had a good deal more at her command than she usually did; the evening with Brock and her daughters had insured that. But she had to be careful around Ronan: her emotions could wreak havoc on any magical help.

Almost immediately the fear melted from Ronan's face, though, and trusting like a lamb, he followed her back inside. Once there, she had his nurse help her run him a bath and after several pots of water had boiled and been emptied into a wooden tub, she asked the nurse to leave them alone. Gently, she undressed him, trying not to look too closely at the grayish skin. It seemed thin as winter leaves, hanging off his bones with nothing to tie them to his body. Like a ghost. Still under her spell, he let her do as she wished. He even closed his eyes for a moment, when she ran her hand down his back. He had loved her hands on his skin before his mind had been shattered, had exhaled low groans that had rumbled in his chest, until he'd clasped her wrist, pulled her into his arms.

The memories stung.

"Ronan?" she asked, just for a moment she sounded as hopeful as a child. But he opened his eyes again and she knew it hadn't meant anything. She led him to the tub, carefully placing first one and then the other of his legs in the steaming, soapy water. He moaned in surprise and distrust, but she talked him down again. When he sat down in it, water reached just over his navel and his knobbly knees stuck out like rocks off the coast.

Maeve picked up a bar of soap and a sponge. She rubbed them together hard, until they foamed and she massaged it into his shoulders and his back. She didn't like herself for it, but she feared his eyes, and it was easier to kneel behind him. In his eyes, all she would ever read again was emptiness and fear.

"You would have liked her," she finally started again, maybe just to hear herself talk or for the tiniest chance that something went through to him somewhere. "She can be stubborn. But she would also do anything for the one she loves... like you. Remember? She's brave, braver than she thinks..."

She blinked away a tear that threatened to run down those alien, wrinkled cheeks she had to wear.

"I know you remember me, Ronan... remember us. I know you do. And I will keep telling you, I will always keep telling you about our love. About that night under the moon when you found me stealing peaches from your estate..." she chuckled sadly but washing the smells away made it easier to wrap her arms around his wet shoulders and kiss his cheek from where she knelt behind him. "You had such a beautiful frown."

Sighing again, she let go of him and washed the soap out of his hair. With a small pair of scissors, she cut the most rampant of his strands away. He once been a man who cared for his appearance and it hurt her to see him forget about it. It wasn't much, but there were small things she could still do.

"Cold..." he groaned hoarsely after a while and Maeve helped him out of the tub, then rubbed him dry. It was such a curious sensation, that strangely aged skin under her fingers. He hummed with pleasure at the touch and gently, she kissed his collar-bone.

"You do remember me... you have to remember me..." She cleared her throat, threw one glance at the closed door to the other room and then, without another breath of hesitation, she let her disguise fall like a worn-out robe.

213

The skin over her cheeks and neck stretched and spanned, her hair came to life, red and flickering like fire as she let the magic run free. So Maeve stood, basked in her golden glow, the same lush body, the same vixen face of old. She had elfin features to the slant of her brows and her ears and a sweetly rebellious glint in her features. She was the same woman he had fallen in love with, and she stared at him, willed him to remember, to love her again.

Ronan held her gaze.

Then he started to scream.

AT THE EDGE OF THE WORLD

A Taste of Winter will be released in October 2014.

If you wish to learn more about Lilt Literary and its releases, please visit:

www.liltliterary.com

Thank you for your confidence in our books!